WEST TO THE
ELEPHANT

D1607601

WEST TO THE ELEPHANT

J. SPRIGLE-ADAIR

authorHOUSE®

AuthorHouse™
1663 Liberty Drive
Bloomington, IN 47403
www.authorhouse.com
Phone: 1-800-839-8640

First published by AuthorHouse   01/05/2012

ISBN: 978-1-4685-4095-6 (sc)
ISBN: 978-1-4685-4094-9 (ebk)

Printed in the United States of America

Any people depicted in stock imagery provided by Thinkstock are models, and such images are being used for illustrative purposes only.
Certain stock imagery © Thinkstock.

CONTENTS

CHAPTER 1

Pigs in New York City

November 15, 1848

"Mama!" I called as I ran up the porch steps. "Do I smell like pig?"

Mama opened the door and I could see her eyes widen and her bow lips press together against a smile. "Want to tell me what got you so riled up?"

"The stupid pigs interrupted my walk with Aden. They snort and grunt and mess on the roadways and sidewalks. It is absolutely disgusting."

Mama gave me that almost imperceptible sigh. She continued peeling potatoes.

"Those pigs and their owners act like they belong right there on the walkways."

"I can't imagine where else they'd be if they are going somewhere."

"Mama the point is, that drifts of hogs being walked through our city are absolutely disgusting. That's the point."

"If we had garbage collectors, we wouldn't need the hogs to eat our food waste. Until then, we have to put up with them." Mama rinsed the potatoes and put them in a pot. She ran water from the faucet. That's when my tears started.

"Emelie, let me see you." Mama pulled me close. "It's the move, isn't it? More than the hogs in our streets. It's about leaving your Aden and our house and everything you know." I nodded. The tears wet my pinafore, and mama's shoulder. She didn't seem to mind.

"It's time for tea and talk, my sweet."

I watched Mama, her skirts plumped out with petticoats, and I wondered if we would dress with crinolines in the west. Mama was shorter than I. I seemed to grow when I reached 12 years. And now, at 14, I am a full head taller. Yet, she seemed energetic to a fault. The fault was that she always asked me to do this or that. The only time I saw her sit and rest was in the evening. Resting to her was knitting, and that only happened at night.

She filled the kettle. Then I watched her remove the cover of a burner to place some sticks inside. Matches along with her breath lit the stove for the kettle's water. She came to sit by me and with her hand holding mine, I put my head on her shoulder.

"I remember the night the move was decided, Mama. I'll remember it till I die. Papa brought home maps made by a man called John Fremont who worked for the Army. I watched him open them carefully and study them under the lamp, tracing some lines with his finger over and over. Something serious was going on in Papa's mind, I could tell. Mama, did you know what Papa was thinking about?"

"Yes, dear, I did." She rubbed my back in a soothing manner as I spoke.

"When he began to bring home books—books about the Oregon and California territories, that's when I put everything together. I even remember the night he set them down in front of us once the supper table was cleared, and shooed away David's hand twice from one of the shiny covers before he spoke to us. Do you remember that, too? He even persuaded you away from dishwashing chores and set you right beside him."

"Yes, dear. Papa was excited, he wanted all of you to realize this was to be a true adventure," said Mama softly.

2

"Mama, I don't care about tall grasses that sway in the wind or mountain ranges with strange names like Sierra Nevada and Rockies, or snow falling as early as October and thick enough to be around until spring. All I wanted to ask Papa was, "What about Aden and me?" And not only Aden, but everything else I love is being taken away from me. What does Papa's own mother think of this travel? Our Nonna will miss us terribly."

"Emelie, Nonna Grandi believes in Papa. She will miss us, but is planning to come out west as soon as we're homesteaded. You must believe in Papa, too."

I sipped my tea slowly. Mama didn't really understand me. She lumped me together with my brothers and little sister.

When our tea was over, I climbed the stairs to my room as though a Western mountain was before me. Slowly, one foot carefully placed in front of the other, holding on dearly to the railing for support, I climbed up. When I found my bed, I fell on it and sobbed until I thought I'd die of heartbreak. I couldn't fathom being three thousand miles from my beloved Aden.

CHAPTER 2

The Last Morning

April 5, 1849

Today is the last morning I'll look out of this window in my bedroom and see my favorite maple tree. We're having a bout of April showers, which seem more like an April torrent to me. The rain is thumping on the tin roof above my head, and the wind is causing some little saplings to lose their new leaves. I believe my tears are flowing as fast as the rain on the windowpane. Next autumn, when the maple's leaves are bright with oranges, yellows and reds, I'll not see them because I'll not be here.

I'm worn out from trying to show my family my grown-up self. I was hoping they'd be so impressed that I'd be allowed to remain behind with Nonna. "Mama, I'd like to help you cook dinner tonight." or "I'll finish the ironing because I did my homework already." I tried to be the perfect daughter. I helped Mama with dinner before she'd ask. I took over the ironing when homework was finished. I braided Cora Jo's hair each morning for school, and asked her to please not yell her head off if I found a knot. I dropped hints about how grand it would be to graduate from the first and only school I had ever been enrolled in.

Being responsible all the time was exhausting. Worse, it seemed no matter what I did, Papa and Mama wouldn't hear of me staying behind. Mama said she needed my help. Papa said this was to be an education beyond anything schools could offer. Of course the real disappointment came when Nonna Grandi said that my place was with my family. I felt like adding, in whatever God forsaken place Papa takes us to. But I didn't.

I'm sitting on the bare floor, looking around this empty room and thinking the life I had here is forever over. I am miserable. I'm angry at Papa.

I hear the outside door squeaking open and a quick scrape on the hemp mat by the door. That's the careless way my brother Stephen wipes his shoes. He's home from his last morning's work at the bakery.

I try to quiet my breathing to overhear what my sixteen-year-old brother is saying about his last morning's work at Lazarra's bakery. My dear Aden works every day along with Stephen. They are both learning to be bakers. Oh, the fresh, hot fragrant bread we've enjoyed!

"They all wished us luck on our adventure, Mama. And Mr. Lazzara gave me all the bread I could carry and cookies, too." Stephen's breathlessness tells me he's been running all the way home from the bakery.

"Emelie! Emelie! Time to be down."

I try to brush some tear stains from my traveling dress, but they are about as stubborn as Papa is about this trip. I turn into the stairwell and descend toward the smell of bacon. But my nose is not getting my stomach ready to eat. I am feeling sick. What I see makes me feel even worse. The table is set like it's an ordinary breakfast on an ordinary day with bacon, eggs, biscuits, and cocoa, all steamy and fragrant.

"Mama!" I want to cry out, "don't make me go." But I'm interrupted. Cora Jo, David and Freckles, our mutt, leap into the kitchen from outside, soaking wet, leaving a trail of water wherever they step.

"Mama, what a good breakfast!" my sister exclaims.

"Umm, smells good," says David, and gives Mama a kiss on her cheek. He sees the bakery sweets. "Stephen, they'll last us 'til California if we ration them right. I'll get on that right now!" David begins to count each one. I cannot imagine cookies giving him such pleasure when our lives are changing second by second.

Cora Jo, still dripping, leans over the baked goods and oohs and ahhs.

"Enough," says Mama. "Change your wet clothes. Papa will be home any minute now!"

When Papa comes in, I keep my eyes down, embarrassed by my tears. We sit and join hands for the blessing. Papa's prayer seems to have a tinge of cheerfulness in it, which upsets me even more. After Papa finishes, I look at the food on my plate. The pile of scrambled eggs looks like a jagged mountain. The bacon, a bumpy trail. The jelly is bright red, like—ugh! I'm going to be sick. I run to the door and lean out just enough so the rain doesn't wet me completely. I retch and then feel a soft touch on my shoulder.

"Come on inside, dear, and have some hot tea. It will settle your stomach."

I turn into Mama's hug. She is warm and safe.

"Mama," I whisper, "Do I really have to go?"

"You have to go," she says quietly. "As long as we're together, things will be fine."

The wagon, about as big as our whole kitchen, begins to roll with a wobble and a groan. We'll be getting on each other's nerves in no time. As I look about me, I remember that our only respite from each other will be our sleeping arrangements. The boys will tent outside with Papa. Mama, Cora Jo and I will sleep inside the wagon. "That arrangement will give us sufficient room to stretch out," says Mama.

I wish Mama would stop making this seem like just another day. Who wants to stretch out on a wooden floor of a wagon?

Josie, our Morgan, gets into a rhythm. David, Cora Jo, and Stephen are leaning out the back straining for the last look at everything familiar. Our neighbors are on the street, umbrellas in hand. Kisses are blown and promises of keeping in touch are made. Even the clouds are crying at our departure. I hear all the babble mixed in with the rain but remain glued to my bench, hoping Mama's sweet tea will not decide to return to my mouth.

I gaze way beyond my sister and brothers into the gray morning when I see a figure running toward us, his arms waving like they were a windmill. My heart jumps when I realize it is Aden. At first his words are muffled until I hear them clear as a bell, "Mr. Grandi, Mrs. Grandi, Emelie, wait!"

It's Aden! I jump up and squeeze myself between Cora Jo and Stephen. "Papa, wait for Aden!" My shouts are lost in the raindrops. My brothers take up the call, and I hear Papa's, "Wait for whom?" as he slows down. When Aden comes close, I jump out into his arms. There, in the sight of everyone, Aden and I hug. He feels very wet but his arms hold me with a firmess I like. He unwraps my hands from his neck and presses a small gift into them.

He smiles his words into my ear, "This will help you remember me," and lets me go.

"Godspeed, everyone!" he calls to my family.

I climb back into the wagon, wet as a fish, but Aden's love is warming me right to my toes. Mama wraps a towel around me without saying a word. I close my eyes to block out everything but that memory. I want it to stay with me forever.

We turn from our street to the highway. I look at the small package. In a wet, wrinkled paper is a small dough heart preserved with an egg-white glaze. On it are crimson-red words that I remember from the Bible. They are from the prophet Ezekiel: I called your name, and you are mine.

I hold it tight and close my eyes. The good times we've had together are filling my brain: Last Halloween when Aden had me cut into a pumpkin pie until I found his ring—and the pie looked like pumpkin pudding! Sitting by the swing in the school yard, sharing lunch, and him making me laugh till I hurt. Last Christmas when we promised ourselves to each other forever at the York Grange Hall, neither of us knew come April we'd be saying goodbye. Will I never again get to brush his bright red hair from his forehead, where it always liked to lie no matter how much spit he put on it? Can I live without the smell of Aden's breath after eating cotton candy at the fair?

As sudden as a shooting star, an idea comes to me. I am going to slip away from this crowded wagon back to Aden, back to my Nonna, and back to the city I love.

CHAPTER 3

Philadelphia

April 5, 1849

Philadelphia looms before us as we bump along in the wagon. It reminds me a little of New York and home. Tall buildings, people rushing to and fro, streets paved with pebble stones all leading to someplace I don't want to be. To amuse myself I check on street names. Back home I'd see *Broadway, Wall* and *Pearl* streets. Here I see street names like *Chestnut, Pine* and *Walnut.* All tree names. Not much thinking here.

"Look at that building. It must be four stories high!" calls David, as he leans out from the back.

"Five stories!" argues Cora Jo.

"I'm counting right now. See, one, two, three, four. It's only four."

Cora Jo sighs, "Well, it's tall, anyway. Emelie, when we stop will you help me groom Josie? Mama said I'd better get busy learning our horses.

"Did you take what we need?"

"Everything. I even have Mama's baking soda to brush her teeth." Cora Jo points and my eyes follow her finger. Of course Josie's grooming items would be there, along with Cora Jo's belongings—little animals that Mama sewed from scraps for each birthday, tiny clothes for the animals, and even blankets for her creatures. Don't know how she even fits on her sleeping mat. Despite all her toys, she's the best in the family at taking care of Josie.

From the corner of my eye, I see Stephen lying on his mat. He waves Papa's itinerary in the air, hoping to get my attention. Finally he sits up with a serious face, like he's more than two years older than me. "Papa has planned all our stops. Tonight our first stop is in an ordinary."

I take a good deep breath, and try to keep my voice down. "Papa, Papa—that's all I hear. Papa decides, Papa wants adventure, Papa wants education for us children. I don't care what Papa wants, I don't want to go."

Stephen is quiet after my outburst. I feel like running away right this minute. I touch the dough heart. It's still there, safe in my bodice.

As we continue bumping along, I remember Stephen's dream of studying engineering at the Rensselaer Institute like Papa did. Now with this move he'll never get there. Why isn't he angry about moving West?

Lately when I see Papa and Stephen together, I've noticed something growing between them that is crowding me out. I don't care. I won't be here long, I'm going back to my Aden.

"Whoa, Josie!" shouts Papa. "Here's the stop everyone's been waiting for! Louisa, children, that's it over yonder. The Philadelphia Hotel. Let's see our rooms before we get the provisions we need for tomorrow's trip."

"Children, Papa and I need to shop. Would you like to come along?"

"Could I just stay here, Mama? I want to brush Josie," Cora Jo pleads.

"I don't want you to stay by yourself."

"David, please stay with me. Come on, please," begs Cora Jo.

David smiles and jumps behind Mama to hide.

"Please, please, Davy."

"Okay. I'll stay. Hey Stephen, would you go back with me later to the mercantile? I want to see everything in this city of brotherly love."

"My Davy. You are so good to your sister," says Mama smiling at her twelve-year-old son, then to us, "Come along now, Emelie and Stephen. Let's not keep Papa waiting."

The walkway alongside the street is narrow. I have trouble walking next to Mama. Sometimes I'm ahead of her and other times, behind. My brain begins to think it may be easy to become lost in this city. I put that idea in a corner of my brain as I notice how difficult it is for wagons to pass without one moving up on the sidewalk. The houses aren't wide either. If not for the different facades of wood or brick, I would have trouble distinguishing one from another.

Vendors' signs appear, some fixed to their front doors, others hanging from a bracket. I'm amused by the pictures on the signs: jackets, pigs, cows, sheep, and milk bottles. We walk on. I see a group of folks waiting for a stage coach. My idea is born. While Mama and Papa shop with Stephen, I'll come back here and be part of the crowd waiting. It will be easy.

Another block and Mama finds the mercantile shop she wants. My heart begins beating wildly. I look at my parents and brother. I touch the dough heart. Yes, I will leave my family here and get back to where I belong.

I wait until Mama and Papa enter the shop. My brother holds the door open and motions for me to enter. He doesn't know what I'm planning. I take a deep breath, and look about me. The colorful trinkets hold no interest. I move over to the clothes. The heavy wools with mother-of-pearl buttons look fashionable. Clothes are so much more useful than jewelry. I twist Aden's ring on my tall finger, and I feel in my bodice for the dough heart. These are the only things important to me now.

In a moment I find myself completely without my family as they begin their browsing. I go to the door, open it and walk out.

CHAPTER 4

Freedom with Fear

April 5, 1849

I run, breathless, back towards the crowd waiting for the stagecoach. When I reach them, I smooth my dress, push back my hair, and wait like I'm an experienced traveler. Only then do I catch my breath and look about. They are strangers, all of them, children with parents, young people returning from somewhere going to somewhere else, old ones anticipating travel, others looking sad, and me.

Now my brain begins to haunt me. I will be alone. A solitary six-hour coach ride back to my home, returning to school after I've said my teary goodbyes, wondering whether Nonna will be welcoming or scolding. These thoughts flow large and dark.

I push them away by remembering how capable Stephen is. He'll take care of everything.

I fiddle with my cloak, buttoning all the buttons, anything to keep my attention from what I'm about to do.

"Can I help you with that, miss?"

I turn toward the voice. The girl looks about my age but she is pale and thin. I believe there is an odor of uncleanliness about her. Yet, her gentleness draws me.

"Thank you. I'm fine, just a bit disheveled from running," I answer, and then I see her put her finger to her lips. She begins to speak again just above a whisper.

"I came because you are being watched by the man standing by the fine wagon. He will want you to go with him and will promise you everything. I'm warning you not to go."

I look out beyond the girl to the man, when she continues.

"I can't let him see me talk to you. I'd better move away, but beware of him and his kind."

She slips away as quietly as she had come. I'm feeling bewildered. I glance at the man again. He is smiling at me. I quickly turn away yet I feel the blood rushing up to my face. He is well dressed like Papa is when he goes to work. His stovepipe hat makes him look much taller than Papa. Am I not safe among this crowd at this stage stop?

I want to find the girl to speak to her about travels without a family, about living in a strange city. I look around me. I move closer to women who are traveling alone hoping to find her there.

The crowd becomes restless as the stagecoach approaches. I don't see her, and it leaves me with a feeling of abandonment. I see him moving closer as the crowd moves toward the station.

A man's voice quiets the group. He tells the crowd that boarding will begin with those who have tickets in their hand. There will be no selling of tickets on the train. I find myself one of the many folks making their way to the ticket counter.

"One ticket to New York City, sir."

"Five dollars, miss."

"I'll have to pay at the other end. You see, my Nonna lives there. She will pay you."

The man laughs so loudly, I become embarrassed. "Didn't anyone ever tell you it cost money up front to ride a train?"

"Why I know that, sir. I just don't have the money now."

"Well, move on then, lassie, no money, no train ride."

"I will pay for her." The voice is deeper than Papa's. When I turn, I see him. That that grinning man! Besides his hat, his formal coat with velvet collar frighten me. My braveness depletes like the air in a balloon after a pinprick.

Run! And I run away from the coach station, the crowd, and the dream of returning home. When I stop, I realize I don't know where I am.

A whiff of something is in the air—pigs? I peer around the corner to see if my nose is playing tricks on me. I only see children playing and grown-ups talking. Don't others smell it? I watch the children. They have a hoop that they are trying to keep up with a stick. Finally they yell, "Pigs, pigs!" and run towards their mamas.

I find a recessed door front and press myself against one wall. Praying for protection from the Blessed Mother, I vow never to leave my family again. My fright of pigs and of that strange man have not awarded me with the best of experiences in this city. I will not be happy, but I best travel with my family.

One comfort achieved. Another distress swells. How do I excuse my absence from my family? What do I say to them?

I no sooner push open the door to the mercantile when the shopkeeper looks up and says to me, "Miss, your folks were looking for you. They seemed mighty worried."

I rush back to the ordinary dreading a confrontation. I'm too embarrassed to tell the truth. I'll think of something, something that hides the truth of my disappearance.

Mama and Cora Jo greet me with hugs.

"Emelie, did you get lost? We couldn't find you after we left the mercantile," says Mama into my hair, as she squeezes me with her love.

I try to mask my anxiety with a forced smile when my sister begins the admonishment I was expecting.

"Papa and the boys are looking for you everywhere. They haven't even returned yet!"

"I wanted to look about while you all were shopping. Then the pigs came down the street. You know me and pigs. Well, I just had to hide somewhere fast. I'm sorry, Mama, I should've told you. I thought I'd be back before you got worried." My lame voice was such a lie, but if Mama didn't believe me, she kept it to herself.

When Papa came home, he was angry and showed it plainly. "No one is permitted to leave without telling someone where you are going. That is strictly forbidden. This is a dangerous trip and we must stay together wherever we are, even if the place seems friendly. Understand?" I nodded but I still couldn't look at Papa although I knew he was looking directly at me.

When the "talk" was over and chores resumed, I found Papa alone looking at his maps. I stood nearby and waited for him to look up.

"Papa, I'm sorry for causing you and Mama such worry. I promise I will not be so foolish as to do what I did today."

"Emelie, we wouldn't know how to carry on if something happened to you."

I hugged him from behind as he still sat on a bench. He patted my hand, and I felt a tear on my arm. I closed my eyes and kissed Papa on his head. I knew then my planning to leave would be a daydream unfulfilled.

CHAPTER 5

Bertie

April 12, 1849

The next morning, Stephen and I load the wagon for the next leg of the trip which will take us to Pittsburgh. I'm still embarrassed in front of my older brother about yesterday's escapade, so I remain quieter than usual. He's brimming with anger towards me. I feel it.

"Emelie, you don't know this, because you're too selfish, but Papa is really worried about this trip. More than he lets on. He wants Mama to decide whether or not to continue in case he should be killed. I already told him I couldn't take care of things the way he'd like unless I had you to help."

"Killed?" I look at my brother with furrowed brow. I can't tell if he's scaring me or if he really means it. "If this is dangerous travel, why is Papa making us go?"

"You know, it's an education, and Papa believes it so strongly that we're going. But back to the topic, please. You know how Mama needs you to help with the women's work. I can keep up with the trip and the map reading, but the niceties of the daily trip, well, that's your department."

I am mute. My brother's words leave me stinging with responsibility I don't want.

Before we're finished loading, Papa comes by to show us a horse he purchased to help our Josie pull the wagon. I see his coat looking like matted cotton, and his teeth are yellow as dried-out Indian corn. Just as I'm ready to check to see if he smells like pig slop, Papa continues.

"With this horse, we should be making twenty miles a day without much trouble," says Papa.

"I guess Papa isn't looking for beauty, he's as ugly as they come," I whisper to Cora Jo.

"That's not nice, Emelie. We'll fix him up, you'll see."

"Starting today, we'll be caravanning with a widow woman who's fulfilling her dream of going west. When you finish currying our new roan, come inside to meet her. Mama's speaking with her now."

I look at Stephen, "Is this a surprise to you? It's not like we don't have a big enough family ourselves, now we have to welcome another woman, a widow at that. She'll probably be filling us with her tears and sorrows, something I don't need to listen to."

"Papa mentioned the safety of traveling with others."

"Oh, yes, I can understand us traveling along with some strong men and boys to protect us against the wild people who live out West, but a widow woman?"

I see her waiting for us in the lobby, standing out like a rose in a wildflower garden. Her heavy brocaded black dress is decorated with white lace at the neck. On her head is a plumed hat of scarlet with wide satin streamers tied under her chin. Her white gloves must be made of young calf, because they look as soft as baby's down.

"Hello. I'm Bertie Wann," she says, and holds out her hand.

Stephen takes her hand first, and bows slightly. She says, "I hope you can call me Bertie. We'd better dispense with the formality because we'll be crowded enough without adding more fences."

She gives both Cora Jo and me a hug and I smell her sweet perfume, like lilacs in early summer. I wonder how long she'll smell of lilacs. There won't be many bathing areas on our way. There is a hint of a British accent about her speech, and her spirit seems very much like Papa's, a ready-to-go-this-minute kind of person. I wonder how long that will last as we get to traveling. I know old folks can't take hardships that young ones can. Do Papa and Mama really know how they will be slowing us down with that woman? And, her dress? Hardly the raiments for travel into no-man's land.

"I see the surprise on your face. That's right, I'm going west. My husband and I always planned to see California. But you know how life is. Things don't always go as planned. My husband caught the ague and died right in my arms."

Bertie takes out a lace-edged hanky and wipes her eyes. "Before he died, my husband made me promise I'd make this trip without him if I had to."

The widow's spine straightens as she gives a tug to her bonnet.

"Well, I have to. So that's what I'm doing. I'm going west." Her eyes sparkle with those words, and she gives me a friendly poke," Just like you, Emelie. We're all going west."

Yes, I thought. We're going west. And I hope you don't spoil it with your tears and finery. Besides, it's still the wrong direction for me.

"Would you like to see my wagon before we leave the city?" smiles Bertie at the four of us.

My brothers and sister answer for me. I have no desire to see the inside of her wagon. It's just a wagon. A horrible, bumpy, uncomfortable wagon. But of course I tag along. I best keep my mouth closed.

We watch her reach to the bench where she places her hat just behind the driver's seat. There, hiding underneath, is the curliest gray and black hair I have ever seen. Ringlets pop up all over her head despite her short haircut and the tightness of her hat around her forehead. She places the hat just behind the driver's seat and begins to remove her gloves, one finger at a time. She chats the entire time without watching what she is doing. When she has freed her hands I notice that they are quite different from Mama's and Nonna's. They seem to be perfectly shaped and well groomed.

We walk cautiously into the back of her wagon. When I see it stuffed with her possessions, I want to snicker and ask her if she really believes she can get all these boxes to California. Doesn't she know we gave a lot of our possessions away? Couldn't she have done that, too?

"These are all remembrances I collected along life's path. Your Mama and Papa have been in here and they, too, marveled that I had so much. But remember, if something is important, one always finds room for it, whether in your heart, your head, or your wagon."

"You have so many trunks, Mrs. Wann," Cora Jo exclaims.

"They are good at keeping things neat and dry. I plan on dressing-up from time to time in that old prairie we're headed to. Never know when we'll be invited to a captain's ball. I want to be ready."

I couldn't help but giggle at that. She was making light of this expedition West, making it seem like it was nothing more than what folks do every day. She's in for a surprise.

"Boys, in this trunk are tools, every kind of tool that strong boys and men might avail themselves of during this trip. Feel free to dig in and find what you need at any time."

My brothers and sister are very quiet; overwhelmed is a better word, as they keep looking at things that catch their eye. I stand quietly, watching them but not moving a muscle to venture closer to Mrs. Wann's so-called treasures.

"Now here's something to remember, and I've already spoken to your parents about this. Anytime your wagon seems too hot, too crowded or one of you just needs 'time alone,' please come and sit with me. I want you to think of my wagon as the second one that belongs to you. Promise?"

Time alone? Yes, I would like that, but I don't want to spend time with the widow woman who would probably want to pry into my private life if I chose to ride with her.

One time I remember clearly, was when I was twelve and my menses started. Knowing that my body could grow a baby within it was such a shock, I had trouble concentrating on school work. I thought I would never be able to walk properly with those rags between my legs. And, the hardest thing of all was that I had to pretend in front of my brothers that nothing was different with me.

Then there was the time last Christmas when Aden and I made a promise to each other to marry soon as I was finished with my studies. After such a loving moment, I walked right into the bedlam which is my family. It would have been nice to have a quiet place to go. Now I do, I just wish it wasn't with her.

The church bells chime ten o'clock as our two-wagon caravan turns and twists through the neighborhoods of this city where my plans got changed. I see the narrow houses, the pretty little gardens in front, people walking to and fro. I feel both a kind of relief and a deep sadness now that I've made up my mind to stay with my family. In my heart I know that Aden is with me forever and ever.

CHAPTER 6

Riding with Bertie

April 13, 1849

Spring has covered the hills in soft green and the dandelions in bright yellow. We have a blue sky and bright sun. All would be at least tolerable if my brothers hadn't decided we should take turns riding with Bertie to help relieve our crowded wagon. And that I should be the first one to ride with Bertie as we set off for Pittsburgh.

So here I sit next to her, thinking of all her things in the rear of the wagon that she can't live without. I have nothing to say. I sit quietly as she drives.

"I know this journey will change us in many ways," she begins. "I'm trying not to think of the big picture, little pieces are easier to digest. Ten days to Pittsburgh, then we get another respite from our travels."

I look ahead, saying nothing. Truth be told, I believe she's a bit wacky.

"You may be wondering why an old lady like me is taking this long trip out West."

I remain quiet, just wishing she would drive the wagon and stop talking.

"It's true I am an old lady, but a healthy one, and I might add, a soon-to-be wealthy one. Yes, soon as I get myself

West and claim rightful ownership of a possible gold mine, I'll be fulfilling my husband's dream. My dear loving Bertie, I miss him so."

"Did I hear you say his name was Bertie? Isn't that your name?" Now I do think she's simple-witted.

"Bertie Wann is what I go by. My late husband's given name was Bertram. Bertram E. Wann. Not being blessed with children, we traveled, studied, and assisted the poor and infirm."

I nodded in understanding, but remained quiet hoping she'd stop. I didn't want to be bored out of my wits the whole time I had to ride with her.

"It all happened quickly. There I was, with plans to travel and no Bertie. One day, as I was going through his personal papers, I found a poem that he had selected for me in case of his demise. When I read it, it sounded like my Bertie speaking to me. I keep it with me always and read it whenever I feel melancholy. It does wonders for me."

"May I read it someday?" I ask, trying to be polite.

"Nothing wrong with right now. You take the reins, I'll go in the back to get it."

Allowing me to take the reins surprises me. I've never driven before. She must be a simpleton.

She emerges with a beautiful wood and jade box. As she opens it, I see it holds papers and jewelry. She riffles through the contents, takes the reins back, and hands me a piece of parchment. I read:

> *Nay, if you read this line, remember not*
> *The hand that writ it; for I love you so,*
> *That I in your sweet thoughts would be forgot*
> *If thinking on me then should make you woe.*

"It's beautiful. Did Bertie write it?"

"No," she says in a soft voice, as if remembering. "William Shakespeare, a poet, wrote it for those in mourning. Bertie did not want me to sit and grieve after he passed away. He wanted me to move on with life. And that's what I'm doing."

"Yes, that's what you're doing," I repeated, not being certain of her yet.

"But, there's more to my story. Money had never been a problem for us, so we speculated. We bought land, sight unseen, in hopes that it would double or triple in value with the opening of the Western Territory."

"Where we're headed?"

"Yes. And the fifty thousand acres of land I own is in the area where gold has been found. Gold lying in brooks and streams. Placer gold it's called. It comes from a vein somewhere in a nearby mountain. It just drifts down there after rainstorms. I'm thinking I own one of those golden mountains. And, dear child, I want to get out there and claim my land before the law changes."

"But laws don't change."

"Oh, yes they do. Laws change to suit the lawmakers. For instance, in the East, women can't own property. As far as I can find out, the Western Territories have not set those laws yet. I want to stake my claim before they do."

"You think they might?"

"Yes, I do. Just last year, in 1848, California was ceded to the United States by Mexico. Did you know that?"

"We learned all that in school. It happened right after the Mexican-American War through the Treaty of Guadeloupe," I said as quickly as I could. I want her to know I'm not as stupid as she may think.

"Good for you, dear. It always pays to know what is going on around you. Well, recently our government has begun to take a close look at all the transactions made before the Treaty was signed. Who knows if the powers that be should decide my treaty is not worth the paper it's written on. But this Bertie is not going to give up anything without a fight!"

Bertie grasped the reins even tighter. Her mouth was set in a straight line. She was quiet for a moment, and I only heard the clip-clop of our horses' hooves.

"I have taken my husband's name, so my identification matches the name on the deed. Many times legal transactions are executed without the people involved. I'm counting on that so no one will know I'm a woman. That would only complicate matters."

"I didn't know things could get so complicated," I said, suddenly feeling a pity for her.

"Here's my other worry. Our country imports foreigners from prisons around the world telling them they will be freed if they stay on the frontier and settle the land.

Who knows what culprit is settled on my property already? Imagine my waving a document in front of a thief, or worse, a murderer, asking him to leave my property. Possession is 90% of ownership. He'd just as soon take a gun and shoot me dead! Once someone is on my land, it'll be near impossible to remove him. The sooner I get out West, the better!"

"Now I understand. Your name is exactly like your husband's, which will help you in acquiring what's yours."

"Emelie, there isn't a day that goes by that I don't thank my dear mother for naming me Alberta. It has been a blessed name for me all these years, but especially now because of my own dear Bertie."

I take the reins again while Bertie puts the wood and jade box in the back of her wagon. Somehow I feel privileged to know about the box. I tell her so.

"Now, Miss Emelie. You must tell me something about yourself. I fear I've dominated our time together with my talk. Let me know some of your secrets."

I don't feel exactly comfortable sharing things with this lady although I know some of her secrets already. I remain quiet.

"Come on now, just being fourteen suggests feelings of some kind. About not wanting to leave New York City? A young boy, perhaps . . ."

The clip-clop and rumble of the wagon become louder. I imagine Aden back home, attending school and thinking of me as I am of him. I want to speak about him. After a time, I do.

"I left my true love behind. Aden. See this ring I wear? It came from a pumpkin pie he made last Thanksgiving. He had me mess up the pie until I found the ring baked inside. We made a promise to marry soon as I'm finished school. Now you know why I didn't want to make this journey. I miss Aden more than anything."

"Tell me all about Aden, dear Emelie. What he looks like, what he does, how you met him, what your family thinks of him. I want to get to know all about him because he's important to you."

"It was yesterday he surprised us just as our wagon was rolling away. He gave me something else to remember him by."

"Do you keep it with you?"

"Oh, yes, Bertie, it's right here in my bodice."

I reach inside my blouse and pull out the dough heart. Bertie gives me the reins and I give her the heart so in seeing it she might understand a bit more about my Aden. She fingers it carefully, turning it around and marveling at the artistry of the lettering on so small a piece.

"It's lovely," she says. "A perfect piece to demonstrate love."

"We met at school. Aden was in my brother's class. He's tall as Stephen. His red hair never stays where he wants it to. It goes every which way even after he combs it. Just thinking of it makes me laugh!

"Our plan was to be together after finishing school. He would continue working in his Papa's bakery and would study to become a master baker. I would work with young children, even teach them, and then we'd marry.

"Of course, we'd like to marry before we finish school like my parents did, but they said that wasn't a good idea. Now with this journey, well, it's useless to speak of marriage with Aden there and me here."

I stop speaking and feel my eyes filling. Without a word, she takes my free hand and gives it a squeeze, just like we are soul mates.

We ride on in silence. I think about Bertie and the purpose of her travel. She is the bravest woman I know.

April 13, 1849

Dearest Aden,

You couldn't know how wretched I've been on this entire trip since I left New York. I napped all the way to Philadelphia hoping it would all be a dream when I awoke. I see it isn't. So much has changed since I left you that I fear you will find me incoherent in this, my first letter, to you.

Since Philadelphia, we became a two-wagon caravan. Bertie Wann is our traveling partner, and we may even grow into a larger caravan before we cross the plains.

We are very close to Pittsburgh now, where we'll get on a steamer and travel down the Ohio River to the Mississippi. Papa wants to rest the horses before the plains, so we'll empty the wagons and stow our belongings on the steamer. Then he and Stephen will have the horses pull the empty wagons to the Mississippi where they'll meet us as we come off the ship. Papa knows how heavy the unloaded wagons are but he says they are a sight less work to pull empty than full.

I wish you were here. Your heart is always next to my own.

Love,

E.

CHAPTER 7

Ten Days on a Steam Boat

April 30, 1849

This morning Papa and Stephen will leave us. I try to hide my melancholy by scurrying around, unloading the wagons and making piles of our belongings on the steamer. I still don't understand Papa's need to separate us to benefit the horses. Aren't we more important than horses? This will be the first time we will be apart. I pray it will be the last. I always feel more comfortable with Papa in charge.

Bertie carries the wood and jade box. I catch her eye and smile. She winks at me. It takes us three hours to unload and clean the two wagons and when it's done, I'm exhausted. I notice that the only thing Cora Jo did was name Bertie's horses, Goldie and Oldie. I don't fuss with her this time. She always becomes immobile at a juncture.

Papa hugs Cora Jo first. He smoothes her hair and hugs her so tightly she calls out, "Papa," and giggles. He can always turn her sadness around. I watch them and try hard not to show my sorrow.

When Papa comes to me for a hug, my plan breaks down. My tears leap out like a gusher. While I fiddle for a handkerchief, Papa says, "Emelie, can you keep your tears from wetting me all over? Folks will think I was sloppy with my soup."

"Oh, Papa," I say, smiling and crying at the same time.

"That's better. Can't have an old teary-eyes in charge of Mama, Cora Jo and David. The tears would blur any trouble that comes a-knocking at the door."

We stand at the rail watching Papa and Stephen disappear into the forest that laid West of Pittsburgh. I wonder if Mama felt this empty when no one could find me back in Philadelphia.

I awake at first light to the chug, chug of the steamboat, a new sound to my ears. The steam engine is shaking the deck as its paddlewheels splash noisily in the Ohio River. I sit up and see black smoke and sparks puffing from the two chimneys. On the other side from where we have been resting, there are sacks of flour, coffee, whiskey, shoes, and boxes of yard goods. I can even see jars of preserved pork.

Cora Jo and David are sleeping in the space underneath my bench. With our coats, cloaks, mufflers and gloves, we have prepared an area that is far less comfortable than a bed, but better than sleeping on hard wood. Mama and Bertie have shared another bench, not far from ours. I don't know how they can sleep sitting up like they do.

I'll wait for my sister and together we'll relieve ourselves in the latrine down below. Today the smells won't be too bad, we're not even one day out, but I dread the rest of the journey. Ten days with everyone using the same pot. Can I train myself to hold everything in until the Mississippi?

When everyone is awake, Mama and Bertie serve us sandwiches, which we'll have for lunch and supper as well. "Bertie, would you read a story to us?" asks Cora Jo, with her mouth still full. "We brought lots of good books."

"It would be my pleasure," Bertie says.

Cora Jo runs to our boxes, throws off the top layer of clothing, and begins reading the titles of the books. When I hear my favorite story, *Frankenstein,* I call out, "that's it" to everyone.

Bertie begins the saga, and we settle into it quickly. As old as I am, I love to be read to. When she stops to catch her breath, I look around and see that a small audience has gathered around us. One young man stands alone. His clothes are shabby and his skin somewhat dark, like he's been in the sun. When I catch his eye, he moves away.

"I hope you don't mind us listening. That story always pulls me in," says a pretty young woman with a starched white blouse and black velveteen skirt.

Bertie smiles graciously, points to me, and says, "It was Emelie who picked out this story. I'm glad I'm doing it justice."

"You picked a good one," she says to me. "Was it hard to choose what to take?"

"Yes, it took us an entire afternoon."

"And a lot of bickering," adds David.

She laughs knowingly. "I had the same trouble. The thought of leaving books behind was torture."

A young man joins her. He's her brother, I can tell. Could there be such a resemblance among my family members? I hope not.

Tim and Susan Holt are both teachers from Pittsburgh. How different they are from my teachers. They smile and chat with us like we were old friends. Perhaps this journey may not be as bad as I thought.

"Is your grandmother the talented reader?" asks Susan.

"No," says David, grinning. "She's a widow woman who's come to travel with us. Her name's Bertie.

"Our real grandmother is back East," I chime in. "She wasn't happy at first about us making this journey. There was much conversation about it, but Papa was firm. He finally convinced everyone, except me. My heart is back in New York City," I confess.

"We know what you mean. We left a lot of worrying folks. If it weren't for Tim, I'd be home in Pittsburgh, getting ready for my classes," says Susan.

We look down the aisle and see Bertie walking towards us with Cora Jo and David. The three of them are holding hands and as they come closer, I see both a tear and a smile on Bertie's smooth face.

"We've got ourselves a "Grandma Bertie" for this trip!" interrupts Cora Jo.

"May I present, Grandma Bertie Wann," David bows low, "who will henceforth be known as "Grandma Bertie.""

"My heart couldn't be more joyful than to be asked to be part of your family. To be picked as a Grandma Bertie is a most special honor. I will try to remain worthy of it," Bertie says.

"Yes, you are worthy, Grandma Bertie," I say, and give her a hug right from my heart.

"Mama, isn't it fun to have a Grandma Bertie on this trip?" asks Cora Jo.

"I couldn't be more pleased. Bertie is already one of us, and now we've made it official," says Mama. "Come, let us join hands in thanksgiving for a new family member."

Tim and Susan join hands, and Mama leads us in a prayer of Thanksgiving, her favorite. Seems as if Mama is always thankful for something.

"What a glorious beginning to our Western adventure," says Susan. "This is bound to be an extraordinary trip."

"We are sitting near the railing. Come by and chat with us anytime," invites Tim. "That is if you can stand the smell of the animals. We'll have to put up with it, like it or not, to reap the reward at the end."

"Are you thinking of a reward as a good education, like Papa is? Honestly that's all he talked about months before we actually left New York City."

"I agree with your father. Adventure, that's the education. And land, and maybe even gold," answers Tim. "Right now, come on over to the railing. There's some gold right here under the water!"

"Placer gold?" I ask.

Tim laughs, "We have to wait awhile for that. Here the gold is fish—bass, trout, walleye—good-eating fish! Ever go fishing, Emelie?"

David answers for me, "Sometimes Papa takes Stephen and me. Then the girls pester because they want to go, too."

"Looks like I'll be teaching you girls. Out here we'll all be craving fish after a few meals of squirrel and rabbit."

"Squirrel? Rabbit?" says Cora Jo, with a look on her face that would scare a witch. "I've never eaten a rodent, and I won't ever, either."

"Well, Cora Jo, there won't be any chicken or pork on our wagon train. How about you, Emelie? What's your favorite of the choices we've got?"

"I'll let you know when I get hungry," I say. "Mama's never cooked them." I kept my disgust and the thought of such a meal to myself.

A loud screech breaks the conversation. We all stop like statues to listen as the boat grinds to a halt, sending everything tumbling and sliding into the railings!

"What was that?" I manage to say, trying to hide both my fright and my anticipation of a damaged boat.

"From the scraping sound, I bet we hit some rocks," says Tim. "I'll go find out."

We are almost finished setting things right when I see that young man again walking by.

"Attention all passengers aboard the Ohio Queen! The river is too low for traveling. We'll be waiting for oxen to pull us back into the channel. We are setting up a gang plank now for your convenience and ease of removing all your belongings to the shore."

"What is the mate saying? We just got settled in this smelly boat and now he wants us to undo everything again? If Papa knew what was happening, he'd be here in a minute. This is an omen, I believe it." I shake my head for emphasis.

"You'll do no such believing, Emelie. Our religion forbids it," Mama warns.

I don't give up my thoughts easily, despite what Mama commanded. This entire trip will be a bad luck venture, I know it. Thankfully, Tim and Susan walk over and the sight of those two friendly folks dissolves my annoyance at this predicament.

"Mrs. Grandi, let us help you unload. Susan and I don't have much at all."

"How nice that would be!" Mama smiles, "Bertie, could you use some help?"

"The good Lord sent you to us, I just know it," says Grandma Bertie. "Seeing one's entire life's possessions strewn about so is nothing short of terrifying. Memories packed into boxes need to be cared for. Let's get to it and we'll be finished before we know it."

I start to lift a box hoping Grandma Bertie is right.

"Not that one. It's too heavy for a young lady. I'll take it," Tim says. "Could this be a box of pots and pans for cooking a most delicious dinner? And this light one, this can go right on top. Could it be petticoats for our pretty girls?"

"Are you peeking at our labels?" asks Cora Jo. "That's cheating, you know!"

"Cora Jo, shame on you for speaking plain to a teacher," chides David. "Besides he can cheat, he's a teacher."

There they go again. "How embarrassing," I mumble to myself. But this time Mama heard.

"David, mind your manners! Tim, please excuse my rambunctious son," Mama says.

"I like a person who speaks his mind, just as long as he's not interrupting my classroom," Tim says. "David, you and I have much in common. We like folks to know what we think. Now, let's get to work."

It is dusk when the boat is empty of people and baggage. I see two sailors leading the deck animals out into the forest toward what looks like a clearing. Cora Jo and David are following them while I look for Susan and Tim.

Their oilcloth large and clean is spread under a tree. They wave and invite me to join them.

"How long do you expect we'll be here?" I ask.

"One guess is as good as another," answers Susan. "Our parents told us to be ready for anything on this trip. It looks like this is our first 'anything.'"

Tim joins in, "It sure is, and it could be worse. So much more is coming to delay us, that this happenstance will soon be forgot."

"Tim, let's play our game with Emelie. She'll better understand what we mean," says Susan.

I look at these two people wanting to play a game out here in no man's land, near a river that ran out of water, and with no idea of how long we'll be camping in the woods. Are they funning with me?

"Okay. You've got to think of something worse than what's happening right now. If you can't, you lose your turn. Susan, you start, I'll go, and then Emelie will have her turn."

"It could be raining."

"We could be hungry and have no food to prepare."

"Our horses could stop pulling our loaded wagons because they are tired," I say thinking of Papa and Stephen who left us so that wouldn't happen.

"We could be surrounded by outlaws who jump on board to rob us."

"We could run out of drinking water."

"We could lose a wagon and have to cram everything inside of one. Okay, I understand. There are worse things than being stranded on this river."

"Yes, and it will be good to remember this game on our journey, we'll be needing it again. Now I'm going to see what David and Cora Jo are up to." Tim smiles as he ups and leaves us.

Tim's curly brown hair is tied with a string and it bobs up and down with each stride. Both he, Susan and Grandma Bertie have a civility in manners that remind me of three fine English teachers.

Susan and I sit for a while. I see families making the best of a poor situation. Mothers and fathers are stretching out on the grass. Children and pets are running and jumping everywhere. My eyes wander to a stand of trees and I see that young man again.

"Let's go see what's happening," I suggest to Susan, hoping to follow him.

Susan and I both get up and brush off our skirts. We laugh because we were not sitting on the ground at all. Then I feel better than I have in a long time. Here I am, stranded on the banks of the Ohio, surrounded by all we own in the world, meeting our new Grandma Bertie and now my new friends, Susan and Tim. I feel for my dough heart. It's there. Everything is fine.

CHAPTER 8

Tim

May 3, 1849

"Guess what, Emelie!" David calls. He is breathless with running. "Grandma Bertie wants to cook squirrel for dinner tonight. I got two with my sling shot and Grandma Bertie wants more. She figures they don't have enough meat on their bones for all of us. And, best of all, she's going to teach me how to dress them!" His voice trails off as he goes on another squirrel hunt. Squirrel for dinner? Jiminy, I'm not THAT hungry.

Soon, Grandma Bertie calls us to watch the butchering. Eight squirrels lie dead as ever, waiting to be cut into pieces. The tools are spread out: A cleaver and three sharp knives for the surgery. David moves from one end of the oilcloth to the other inspecting everything. My stomach is churning.

"Ready now, Davie? Watch and follow what I do," calls Grandma Bertie.

Tim is right there near David. They will both be helping Grandma Bertie.

David feels for the first joint above the feet. He severs the feet. He feels for the first joint below the skull. He severs the head. There is blood on the oilcloth, on his fingers, on the knife. I can't watch anymore.

Cora Jo is beside herself with groaning. She puts her hand up to cover her eyes, but I see her peeking out between her fingers every now and then.

"You did well, Davie. Now we're ready to remove the innards."

I begin to watch again. It's horrible, yet I can't take myself away.

David makes a slit in the skin of the stomach from the forelegs to the hind legs.

"Now pull out everything you can. It may seem stuck and slippery, but get a good hold on it and pull!"

Tim moves closer to join David. "C'mon Davie, pull that handful out!"

A slimy, red, mass of stuff comes spilling out of David's hand.

"I'll never eat meat again," cries Cora Jo. "It's too bloody."

I keep swallowing to keep whatever is in my stomach down, where it belongs.

"C'mon girls, watch closely now. We'll see what the organs look like. You'll be pleasantly surprised because they're not bloody." says Tim.

Soon slippery little things are being separated from the intestines by Tim's skilled fingers. "We have the livers here and the kidneys here. And right here are the hearts and lungs," he says as he lines them all in a row.

"This is what you teach your students when you are a biology teacher. It's an anatomy lesson," says Susan to me. "Tim uses frogs at school. It doesn't matter, though, because all critters are pretty much the same inside."

"Okay, David, next we get to pull the furry skin away from the meat. It's called "skinning." Hold the squirrel firmly and pull. Hold it there! Now pull with your other hand so the fur comes off the hind legs."

When Tim sees David getting nowhere, he steps in to help and they both laugh as they struggle to get hold of the slippery rodent. Finally we see the plumpness of the breast.

"Now we separate the legs from the torso, and we are finished! Together you and I make a great team, David," says Tim, and David beams.

I turn to look for Cora Jo. I find her retching behind a nearby tree. "You don't have to eat any of it, Cora Jo. Shall I get Mama?"

She shakes her head "no." I take her hand and walk her back to the campsite.

Quickly as I can, I catch up with Tim and Susan and David and Grandma Bertie discussing the preparation of our dinner.

"Tim, are you really a butcher only pretending to be a teacher?" I ask.

"I suppose I could get hired as a butcher, but then, so could David and Grandma Bertie!"

"Now," says Grandma Bertie, with pleasure on her face, "Remember, the washing is as important as the dressing. All the blood must be washed off or it will curdle our stew."

Susan and I follow Tim and David to the river with the bucket of cut-up squirrel.

"Let's go upstream where the water is cleaner," calls Tim to us.

We all bunch up close to Tim on the river bank. It's time to hear another one of his "lessons." This time he tells us about his hand-carved lures. While we wait, he pulls some out of his pockets.

"Do they really help catch fish?" asks David. "Papa and I always use night crawlers."

"Night crawlers are the best, but when you want to eat without first digging for worms, these do the job. Tell you something. You can each choose a lure to keep. Take one for your brother, Stephen, too. If your lure doesn't catch fish for you, you can give it back, but if it does, you must share what you catch."

"Good deal," says David. "I think I'll catch a big one with this big hook."

"Tim, this one has four small hooks on it. Does that mean I'll catch more than one fish at one time?"

Tim laughs, "Could be, Emelie. Fishing is all about being surprised. Never know what your catch will be. Wait, we forgot about Cora Jo. Can't leave her out. Want to pick one for her?"

David picks a small one for Cora Jo. It has two hooks on each side. "Why do they have eyes painted on them?" he asks.

"They're supposed to look like other fish. You know, if they look like themselves, they can't be predatory. At least that's what we hope the fish think," says Tim.

The water bubbles over some smooth stones where we stop. Tim and David take the squirrel parts from the bucket and carefully lay them on the stones. First they wash the blood from the bucket. Piece by piece they rub blood off the squirrel parts until the outside skin is taut, shiny and smooth. The pieces remind me of tiny baby mice, just born. Rodent, I turn over in my mind. We are going to eat rodent.

"Now what?" asks David.

"Now we go back to our camp and make a delicious stew so your sisters forget this is squirrel."

"Tim, I'm not sure I'll ever forget what this is," I say, shaking my head.

Before we begin our walk back to camp, Tim drops down to drink some of the cool, clear water of the Ohio River. I watch the minnows flee as he drinks in long gulps, their rainbow scales making them look like jewels.

Back at camp, the talk is all about cooking those pitiful squirrels. I believe I'll be like Cora Jo and refrain from dinner. This is the time for a walk by myself.

I head down to the busy part of the river bank. Folks have assembled to watch sailors trying to lift the steamer from the rocks that beached it. The talk is about the possibility of us being here for several days. This has to be the most terrible predicament we've been in since leaving home. I run back to our camp to tell the news I just overheard.

Before I realize what's happened, I find myself flat on the ground. "Oooh," I groan, as I see a bloody tear in my pantaloon. I manage to move into a better position for standing up, when a hand reaches down to help me.

"Thank you so much," I say, embarrassed to see the young man I have seen before on this trip. I feel the blood rush up to my face.

"Hope you didn't get hurt. You sure took a flop," he says.

"It's okay." I say quickly, wishing to die right on the spot. As I rush back to our camp, I smell the fragrance of many suppers cooking. It helps take my mind off my embarrassment.

When we are seated, Mama serves the portions. I remember my manners and don't complain. I find the sweet carrots and onions and eat them first. Next, I find the potatoes and turnips. I push the rodent meat around in the cream-colored gravy. David's mouth is always full. Cora Jo only eats bread. I spear a piece of meat. I hold my breath and put it into my mouth. Thank goodness for the bay leaves and thyme! It actually tastes good.

"May I have more bread to soak up this gravy, Mama?" I ask, finally getting into this meal. I remember Tim's game. It could be worse!

I wake in the middle of the night to loud shouting. It's bad enough to be sleeping on the hard ground and be freezing to death without all this noise. I get up, pull my sweater around me, and creep down to the river. Half-naked sailors, their skin all shiny with sweat, are cursing their labor. Long poles push and pull in tandem with the oxen.

Straps beat down on them to keep them moving. An ox is bleeding, but the beating continues. The steamer creaks and groans until I see her floating free in the main current of the Ohio. I lie down again on my primitive bed, satisfied that the obstacle has been overcome and that soon we'll be loading the steam boat once more.

Noises become louder, and when I see Tim and David bringing logs to the waterfront, I remain to watch the activity. This time sailors are fastening logs together like a raft, except one end of the raft is securely attached to the gangway. It must be an extension to the gangway, which is now too short for loading.

When the gangway is ready, reloading begins. Bags and boxes and Grandma's trunks. Tim looks as tired as I feel, but we all keep to it until the work is done.

I no sooner sit down with Cora Jo when Mama calls, ""Emelie, come help! We're letting Tim and David rest a while. After helping build the gangway and loading, they are dog-tired. Would you fetch water from the stream over yonder?" Mama calls.

Why do I have to go to the stream with all this Ohio River water next to us? But I do as Mama says. When I return, Tim is stretched out on the deck, sleeping like a newborn despite the last-minute activity going on around him. He sleeps through our meal of dried beef, bread and dried apples. As the boat shoves off, quiet descends upon us like a soft blanket.

Late in the afternoon, Tim awakes feverish and crampy. He is thirsty, and Cora Jo and I carry the dipper from the water barrel to his cup innumerable times. "It seems to go right through him," Mama notices, "without hydrating his organs. Time for the laudanum."

"Just a spoonful, Tim," says Susan, and she lets it dribble into his mouth. He retches then vomits. I turn away.

Soon Tim rubs his middle, like it hurts.

"Let's keep him cool until his fever breaks," Mama tells us.

"Moist compresses will do it," says Grandma Bertie.

"Children, find our mended sheet and rip it into sections. Then wet it so we can keep the fever from burning him up." I hear worry in Mama's voice.

Once or twice Tim opens his eyes. I get close to his face and smile like it's okay. I even whisper, "Tim, it could be worse," but I never get the feeling he is looking at me or understanding what I say.

Mama asks Susan if Tim has been ever been ill like this before. I listen, hoping she says that this has happened before and will soon pass.

"No, Mrs. Grandi, I can't remember Tim ever sick. I've been ill with congestion, but never Tim."

Mama tells me to ask the ship's crew for a blanket. When I return, I see Tim shivering like we're in the middle of winter. Mama takes the blanket, pulls it up to his chin, and tucks it under him. Susan rests her head on his chest and puts her arms around him to add more warmth.

When Grandma Bertie and Mama notice tiny beads of sweat appear on his face, a look of relief spreads over them. "The fever's broken," Mama says, "now let's give him an alcohol rub to continue cooling him."

They each take an arm, push up the sleeves quickly and begin to rub before the bad smell evaporates into nothing. Then they pull his sleeves down and cover him again with a light sheet. Mama and Grandma do this many times. We stay close, alert to any command. Suddenly, Tim's breathing stops.

"Tim, Tim, do you hear me?" shouts Mama into Tim's face. Then she slaps him on both cheeks. "Wake up now, Tim. Wake up."

Grandma Bertie rubs Tim's chest, his arms and legs. "Mama, do something!" I shout. I run over to him and grab an arm. "Come on, Tim, wake up. We're here!" I turn to Mama as I continue to shake Tim's arm. "Make him breathe, Mama, please make him breathe. Grandma Bertie, do something. We must do something!"

Mama doesn't look at me. She stares helplessly at Tim. When I see her tears spill out, I know Tim is dead.

What do people do when a loved one dies? I watch Susan to learn. She smothers his face with kisses. "I love you, dearest brother," she whispers. Her head goes down on his chest, while her arms still hold him tight. She sobs like I've never seen anyone do before.

I go to her first, my tears streaming down my cheeks, and gently move her away from Tim. She comes into my arms easily. I rock her and hold her like Mama so often did with us. We cry in each other's hair. I feel her tremble under my hug.

"The cholera?" A passenger calls out, looking at us.

Mama blanches. "I doubt it," she says. "He just fell ill this morning."

Despite Mama's denial, passengers begin moving their belongings away from our small group. We stay huddled around Tim, not knowing what to do next. He looks like he's sleeping.

A sailor comes to us and tells us the captain will anchor early the next morning so graves can be dug. There are three passengers lost to cholera since we reloaded the ship.

Cholera. I've heard of it. Where does it come from? How come my family was spared?

When I see Mama alone, I go to her. I need a hug as much as she. "Mama, is it really cholera? What are we to do?" I'm trembling now. The uncertainty of this trip is so much more than Indians and wild animals and rivers that change names. Disease is now among us. I've heard that cholera is God's way of punishing us. I can't stop my shaking.

"It must have been the water, child. We must always be certain the water is pure before we drink it." Mama keeps looking at Tim like she doesn't believe this has happened. "Let's pray the rosary." She pulls the tortoise shell prayer beads from her pocket and leads us in prayer. I hear my voice, but my head is somewhere else remembering Tim. When we finish, Mama and Grandma Bertie carefully wrap Tim in the blanket that never warmed him and now becomes his shroud. His arms and legs are heavy as we move them to place the blanket around him.

The evening is the longest I ever remember. We sit by Tim's body, none of us sleeping. By the time we anchor and crew and passengers file off with shovels in hand, I become aware of wailings in other parts of the deck. Mournful sounds. I watch the men select a burial site on a hill overlooking this deadly river. The Ohio River only pretends to be pristine. Is this the way Western rivers are? I'll never trust them again.

Sailors return to the deck for Tim's body. We follow them and hold on tight to Susan, knowing that she needs the consolation of our touch. We are silent. There is nothing to say.

I struggle not to watch the ceremony. I want to find something to make my heart sing, like Tim did. Sunshine streams through the maple leaves. I see the moving patterns over the graves, light and shadow, dancing, chasing. I look up. Bright green maple leaves against blue spring sky. White puffy clouds move quickly. There is a tickle on my arm. I look down and see a bug trying to crawl over my arm hair. It falls sideways, but rights itself quickly, its miniscule legs working hard. I see its head and body move in a straight line as if there are no obstacles. Again it tumbles on its back, legs waving furiously. I keep it on me until this burial is over, then carefully, I set it down on the grass. It will never be aware of the giant it crawled over. This is a good place. I know Tim's spirit is here.

The graves are left unmarked. We do not want Indians to dig up these corpses for clothing. At the end, we return to the steamer, holding hands. Mama says quietly, "Dear Lord, we pray we shall not be touched like this again."

I feel my insides tingling with fear of death. I stay close to Susan and watch how Mama and Grandma Bertie, each in her own way, tend to her. Mama offers her foods for nourishment, hot tea for liquid, sweet dried fruit for energy. Grandma Bertie offers her the chance to talk about her beloved brother.

Susan doesn't eat or speak for two days. She sleeps and weeps silently most of the time. I hug her in silence. I watch her when she sleeps. I think sleep is healing her, little by little. The world will be a strange place for Susan without Tim.

One day Susan comes back to us. She takes Mama's tea and speaks about Tim. As she talks, I feel like I've known him for all my life. Yet it was just a few days. Steamboat of sadness, move on. I'm ready for St. Louis.

May 6, 1849

Dearest Aden,

We made some friends on the steamboat and now we lost one of them. Tim died of cholera, although Mama denied it to other passengers. It has such a stigma attached. Some people believe it is God's way of punishing the dissolute among us. I can't believe that. Tim was so good to all of us. Susan, his sister, is beside herself with grief. She'll be returning home to Ohio now that she has lost her brother and traveling companion.

Mama's inclined to think cholera comes from water that isn't pure. She has become even stricter about where our drinking water comes from. There was only one dipper at our water barrel on the ship. We're supposed to dip the water out into a vessel for drinking, but I've seen some people take a quick drink from it when they think no one is looking. I'm glad I never took a drink from that barrel. I've decided that being thirsty is in one's head.

We're off the steamboat. We're waiting for Stephen and Papa to come for us. I can't wait to see them.

Love,

E.

CHAPTER 9

St. Louis

May 9, 1849

"Children," Mama calls, "let's stay together. Papa and Stephen might find us more easily." David sees them first and begins waving his arms and shouting. I'm so happy to see them that his commotion doesn't embarrass me.

Papa has hugs and kisses for us all. Even Grandma Bertie. Stephen gives me a hug. That must be a first for him.

"How did the boat trip go?" asks Papa.

"Papa, so much has happened since we saw you. Mama, tell him. Tell him about Tim and Susan." Although it's always in my mind, when I hear others speak about Tim, my eyes begin to fill.

We sit close together. Mama, Papa and Grandma Bertie sit on a log, while the rest of us sit on the ground. I want to hear Mama tell the story of Tim and dear Susan again. I want to remember it, every detail. I want to see in my mind's eye how two dear people came into our lives and left again.

"It was best that Susan return to her parents," Grandma Bertie says, after Mama recounts the story. "She needs to grieve with them and return to the life she's always known. Being among folks she grew up with helps with the sadness she's feeling now."

"I'm sorry I never met Susan or Tim," Papa says. "They did much to prepare you for what may come next in our travels. It's never easy losing a dear one. We hope we stay blessed with good health. That is the one thing that can make a success of this journey."

We all remain quiet.

Papa begins again. "St. Louis is where the wagon trains form for the Western journey. Stephen and I talked about becoming part of a larger wagon train. We believe it's good for safety reasons."

We work together reloading the wagons. Back and forth we go, calling and shouting about where things should be placed for the most comfort. We gather for dinner in a large dimly lit tavern. There is no printed menu, but the waiter comes over to our table and we listen to the selection of the night. We all agree that this is the place for bison, and then Papa orders dark ale for himself and Stephen. Is my sixteen-year-old brother actually getting a tankard of ale for himself?

"Eugene, what is this? Has Stephen grown up in the fortnight you've been gone that you allow him to have ale?" Mama says.

"Trust me, Louisa. Our boy drove Bertie's horses, helped set up camp at night, sniffed out impending rain, and even cooked some meals, although not as refined as David's, I'll wager." I see Papa wink at David. "Surely he deserves a man's drink."

As Papa's words tumble out, Tim's memory covers me like a spring rain. I remember that meal under the stars like it was yesterday: the dressing of the squirrels, the trip to the river to wash the meat, the lures Tim gave us.

Papa and Stephen raise their glasses of ale and we all follow holding our water glasses. "Let this toast be to the memory of Tim. With God's help, we will continue his legacy."

I touch Aden's dough heart in my bodice. I hope it brings us as much good luck as I pray Papa's toast will.

The next day, as I walk to the post office with Aden's letter, I wonder about him. I wonder what he's doing, what he's thinking and if he thinks of me. I only wish I could speak with him a moment or somehow receive a post from him. But that is a dream for now. We are wanderers. We have no address. I must wait for California.

The frame buildings that make up St. Louis are unpainted, which gives them a frontier look. None taller than two stories, they seem to have been built hurriedly compared to New York's. A boardwalk keeps my feet out of the dirt, but how careful I must be walking these ill-fitting planks! No engineer made this, for sure.

I look up and see the young man who helped me when I tripped over planks.

"Hello. I'm walking more carefully, this time, you see."

"Yessum. I saw you on the steam boat. Are you on your way West?"

"Yes, we are. Perhaps I'll see you again on the Trail."

"Yessum."

He leaves and I continue my walk.

"We are one of seventeen wagons starting the trip tomorrow," Papa tells us during dinner. "It'll be good to travel in a large group. We'll be less vulnerable to attack.

"Tonight after dark the men will meet to draw up an agreement. We need to have some rules for traveling."

"Can we go, too?" I protest to Papa.

"You can all come, if you remain quiet. There will be important discussions taking place. We won't have time for interruptions."

The late May evening is warm and bugs flit around the fire like bees to a hive. The boys, Cora Jo and I walk with Papa to the campfire circle.

"Papa, why do Cora Jo and I have to sit here in the background while you and the boys sit near the campfire?"

"That just the way it is, Emelie. This is a man's discussion."

"Why can't we listen to what's going on? Or even ask a question? Why do we spend so much time in school if we can't be part of an important discussion?"

"This isn't the time or place, that's why".

I take a look at the group that I cannot be part of. Men are leaning against tree trunks. Others huddling near the fire. That young man is also sitting near the men. Being a male is certainly to be of privilege. That's the message I got from Bertie, and now here it is again.

Cora Jo and I become restless at not being able to hear the discussions, so we walk back to the campsite and wait for Papa and the boys.

Papa is tired when he returns. He tells us the new rules for wagon travel. We listen eagerly. "Each wagon will have a turn being in the lead, after which it will return to the end of the train. Day by day, it'll work its way up to the front again.

"The main rule has to do with alerting others of trouble. We all have to have a kettle hanging from our wagon and an iron spoon for banging on its side. Soon as you hear that clanging sound, you're to continue the alarm. That will stop the train, no matter how far the wagons are spread from each other.

"We're going to have a scouting group each day to ride ahead of the wagons. Two men will go together to make sure the Trail is safe for the rest of us.

"Now, about the children, that means you, Cora Jo and David. You are to stay inside the wagon, or if you must walk, keep near the wagon. No hanging off the sides; it is too dangerous with all the animals keeping a steady pace. We don't want any broken bones around here. And tomorrow we will add to our menagerie."

"What do you mean, Papa?" asks Cora Jo, delighted with a word that that suggests animals.

"I mean we'll be getting ourselves some pulling oxen and mules," says Papa. "So everyone to bed now! Tomorrow's a big day."

Our sleeping arrangements are simple: women-folk inside the wagons, men outside in a tent. Cora Jo chooses to sleep in Bertie's wagon this evening.

It's late when Papa creeps from our wagon into the tent where the boys are already sleeping. I lie awake. Mama's breathing becomes regular and I know she's asleep. I hear the crickets noisily talking to each other. I'm as wide awake as they.

We are up early this morning. Oxen? Mules? We're going to have a circus parade all the way to California!

"Papa, are we still going to keep Josie and Brown, although they won't be pulling?" Cora Jo asks.

"We need our horses for riding. Oxen and mules are for pulling and toting. They are not fussy about what they eat. They don't mind dried grasses. You know Josie won't touch anything that isn't bright green."

"Unless it's hay or oats, or carrots, or apples, or sugar!" says Cora Jo, smiling like she got one over on Papa. She waits for Papa's smile and is not disappointed. She continues, "Mules are stubborn. Why do we need them?"

"That's exactly why we need them. They never give up. They are sure-footed, too, and with that combination we can pack them with heavy loads, send them up a rocky incline, and they'll persist until they've reached the top."

A weather-beaten rancher approaches. His brown cheeks have deep crevices and he greets us with a toothless smile. Everything about him seems like it has baked in the hot sun for years. Before Papa says a word, he speaks.

"These here oxen are young and easy to train. Good fer ya purposes. They'll tote up a good load fer ya, too. Looky here, they got some straight limbs. Ya won't have problems on the Trail with these straight limbs." He slaps an ox, tips his hat, and leaves us alone to do our own thinking.

"He sure read our minds, didn't he, Papa?" I ask.

"I think he's seen folks like us before," says Papa.

Stephen and I walk together looking over a few other oxen with straight limbs. We pat, stroke, speak to, and gaze into their large brown eyes. Cora Jo and David find two they like. Soon we are the owners of four oxen. It takes less time to select the mules. They are ornery as can be, so we can't get affectionate with them.

"Let's give them all names," says Cora Jo.

"Slow, slower, slowest and slowness!" calls Stephen.

"No, I don't like those," says Cora Jo. We'll just have to think about it."

"C'mon you big ox," David calls to the one close to him. But the big ox doesn't move. None of them do. We push and yell and slap the reins against their flanks, and finally they mosey on into camp.

Cora Jo and Papa work with the mules, which are about as stubborn as they come. They have been named Maisy and Milo by Cora Jo and we have the task of packing them: one with cooking utensils, the other with tenting equipment. That done I'm exhausted, but Papa isn't. He calls us together to listen to the way we'll be traveling.

"We're going to follow the Missouri to St. Joseph. After a short stop there—a day or two maybe—we pick up the Little Blue River that will take us to the Platte River. Two forts are on the Platte, and we'll stop for provisions. Fort Kearny is first, then Fort Laramie, after which we look for the Sweetwater River. We'll follow it to the South Pass of the Rockies."

"How long will that take, Papa?" asks Stephen.

"I figure about two months," answers Papa.

I'm too mesmerized to even think of time. Is it now that the Indians will appear? Will we see more deadly rivers? Will our horses find the grasses they need? Will our new animals be able to make the trip? Will we? Dear Aden, I wish you were here with me.

The next morning I awaken refreshed and listen to the sounds of morning out here on the prairie: pots clanging, pleasant voices speaking softly, and birds singing sweetly. Cora Jo must be walking around the wagons because I don't hear her outside with Mama.

"Mama, is it okay if I find Cora Jo and walk around with her?"

"Fine, Emelie. Now don't you two get lost doing your investigating. Papa and the boys are with the oxen and mules over yonder. I hope they are better behaved today."

I walk slowly, inhaling the early morning fragrance around me. Food always smells better than it tastes! There's bacon, fry bread and coffee. Everyone cooks the same food out here. My eyes search the wagons behind ours. No sign of my sister. I notice how some folks have hung belongings on the wagon sides. Some have fishing poles, others tools, still others have their gun racks and guns for all to see. Everyone now has a kettle hanging, as Papa says, for an alarm. I look and listen but do not see hide nor hair of her.

When I reach the last wagon in the lineup, I see my sister playing with small children.

"Cora Jo! Come on back, it's time to eat!"

"Can I bring Sarah's tykes with me?" Before I answer, she asks the children if they would like to breakfast in another wagon, then she peeks inside the wagon to ask their mother.

Sarah Robb smiles at our request and says we can have her children any time we wish. "This wagon gets smaller day by day, "she says. "Please don't be strangers. This is a long trek and friendliness will save us from its drudgery."

The children hop, skip, and run back to our wagon with Cora Jo in the lead. I hope Mama and Grandma Bertie will not be too upset at the crowd coming for breakfast.

Breakfast over; we begin our journey in the quiet of the late morning. I watch the mist being pulled off the ground by the sun's warmth. The oxen are slowly moving our treasures along the Trail. They have been named, Anoa, Aurochs, Gaur and Zebu by Cora Jo. I feel like this may be the beginning of a new adventure.

A Thief Among Us

June 10, 1849

The rain awakens me. It is coming down heavy and strong on the canvas cover of our wagon. The wind finds the kettle hanging near the back of the wagon and as it sways, it bumps into Mama's pot. Just as the noise settles down, I feel the outside air blow on me. Something cold and wet slips down between Cora Jo and me. It smells like Stephen. And it is! Having thoroughly wet us, he is now asleep in the warmth of our mats. I would protest but we're all somewhat uncomfortable here in the wilds.

I hear Mama say, "That surely is a gale out there. Did the wind take down the tent, Eugene?"

"Just about. We never dug a trench to catch the runoff from the canvas, so we flooded out."

"Mama, do you have anything to eat in here?" asks David. "I'm starving."

"No, and hush up so the others may sleep."

"David, come here," I whisper just loud enough so he can hear.

"We just got flooded. And now I'm not sleepy. Want to look at my pebbles with me? I carry them with me just in case."

"Just in case what?" I ask.

"Just in case I need them. C'mon, let's take a look."

"It's too dark to see anything."

"We can feel them. I just want to be sure they're all here."

"Who would want to take your silly pebbles?"

"Anyone. They sparkle. Feel this one. It's my skipping stone. It's flat and smooth. Know where I found it?"

"Nope."

"In our garden. Probably long ago there was running water where our garden is and the water made it smooth."

"It does feel smooth. Water did it? Are you sure?"

"And this, this is my mica rock. When the sun shines on it, the mica sparkles. It looks like a jewel good enough for Mama's ring. I found it on the way to school."

"I don't think I ever saw this in the daylight."

"And here's my marble. Well, I think it's a marble. It has a blood-red vein running through it."

We both hear a muted sound. Horse's hooves. We stop talking. Papa moves the flap aside, and we see shadowy figures quietly treading over the mud and puddles.

"I heard the Shoshones expect payment from the whites who cross their land. But we're in Pawnee country now and I don't know if they expect the same," Papa says.

"Papa, they're circling us. Think they want to see how large a group we are?" Stephen is alert now.

"Go inside the corral and make sure the horses are all right. Bring me Brown. I'll alert the others. Do it quietly. David, you wake Grandma and Cora Jo. Bring them here to our wagon."

Papa leaves quietly on Brown to rouse the other men. With an oilcloth pulled over his head and shoulders, he looks like a shadow himself.

When Grandma Bertie and Cora Jo arrive, Grandma is her old jolly self despite this happening. "Today, dear ones, is the day I pull out my gun. I'll be ready for trouble when it comes."

Grandma looks so funny in her nightgown with a shawl pulled over it in a haphazard way. She put on a hat, but it's not near as nice as the one she had on when we first met. This is probably her rain hat. It has only a black veil covering the top of it. But it ties nicely under her chin.

We try to get comfortable in this chilly wet wagon. David shows his stones to Grandma Bertie and we all listen to him again.

Papa returns with good news. "No need to worry," he says as he sits down unaware of the puddle he's making. "They're Pawnee. They work as scouts for the Army. I found out there's little chance of us meeting up with hostile Indians until we're west of Fort Kearny."

"I'm so relieved," says Mama.

"Well, that's good news, if I ever heard any," Bertie says. "Now that I'm up and raring to go, would you young ones like a lesson in predicting the weather? We're bound to have more downpours as we travel."

I don't know what to expect, except that Bertie will make it fun. We follow her back to her own wagon, like she was the Pied Piper.

We fold the sleeping mats and stow them along the inside of the wagon, giving us more room to sit.

"Now, I will pull out all my weather forecasting equipment. I keep most of it right here in this trunk."

"Bertie, can you really forecast the weather?" asks David.

"With my stuff and things and whatchama doodles." Grandma roots around in the trunk. We're very quiet, as she moves things aside and mumbles merrily. "Here 'tis!"

"A pine cone?" Stephen asks. He is as surprised as I.

"Spruce. And here's the other one." She pulls out a matching cone. "Actually, a cone from any conifer would suffice. These were in my yard back home in Massachusetts. When bad weather is on the way, they close up tighter than a drum. In fair weather they open wide."

"To let the sunshine in?" I say.

Grandma laughs. "Now let's put our thinking caps on and find a good place to hang our barometers."

In no time, we have the cones tied with thread and hang them up wherever we find an outside snaggle. They look closed up as they can ever be!

"Gather round, children. That's not the end of it. I've got some sayings you can keep inside your pretty little heads that'll help when you don't have spruce cones to look at.

> *Red sky at night, sailors delight.*
> *Red sky at morning, sailors take warning!*"

"But we're not sailors, Grandma Bertie," says Cora Jo.

"No, but the sky's the same whether we're on the land or the high seas. And it's not only the sky that tells us what's coming but the wind, too.

When the wind is in the East,
'Tis neither good for man or beast.
When the wind is in the West,
Then the wind is at its best.

"And now you've got all you need to forecast weather. You didn't imagine it would be so easy, did you?" says Bertie, mirth creeping over her face.

The sun begins to peep out from under the clouds, and we leave Grandma's wagon to stretch a bit, avoiding the puddles.

"Now we'll watch the cones open up, right, Grandma?" David asks.

"You are a bit impatient, Davey. The air has to dry before it dries the cones, then we'll see a change," answers Grandma. I can tell she's pleased with David's interest. "And for those of you who are so inclined, there's more I'd like to impart. Now that we are travelers together, it may be wise for us both to know remedies for ailments we may develop on the way. A walk to the pond is in order next. See if you can make it without drowning in one of the puddles left by the downpour."

We skirt the puddles of water as carefully as we can. They are all sizes, depths and shapes. I stand over one to see my reflection and am horrified at my untidiness. I surreptitiously look at the others. They don't seem as travel beaten as I. I must wash my hair tonight, no matter how rainy it becomes. I wish Mama or Cora Jo had told me how bad I look. I'm more than happy Aden is not here to see what's happened to me so far on this journey.

The water is muddy, no washing in these puddles. I rack my brain to remember what we may need from this muddy water. I think I've got it! I whisper my idea to Bertie.

"You guessed it, dear one. Leaches are what we need. First identify the oldest puddles, if you can. Then feel around in the murky water."

"Find one? What are you talking about? A fish?" asks David.

"No, a leach," I call out. "Bertie wants us to find a slimy leach."

"What is it for?" Cora Jo asks.

"To help you stop bleeding, or for blood poisoning, whatever ails you that has to do with blood," Grandma answers. "It will be good to have around when we need it."

"Can we take it with us?" David asks.

"I don't know how long he can live out of water. Emelie, remember the bottle under the driver's bench? Would you get it for us? We can put our leach and some pond water in there and take it with us. Davey, would you like that?"

David smiles his approval, and I dash back to Grandma Bertie's wagon for the bottle.

The wagon looks different. Did we forget to pull the canvas when we left to walk to the pond? I jump up to the driver's bench and find what was stowed under the benches is now strewn about. I pull open the cover and peer in the back. A disarray of hats, clothing, bedding, and boxes confronts me.

I run back to the pond yelling, "Mama, Grandma Bertie, come quick, someone's been in the wagon!"

CHAPTER 11

A Puzzle

Still June 10, 1859

"People figure out where folks hide things," is all Papa says about Grandma's valuables.

"Is it someone traveling with us?" I ask, afraid of the answer.

"More than likely. With the Pawnee coming in on horseback and the men meeting with them, the men are accounted for. With Grandma Bertie and all of you down at the pond, the empty wagon looked like fair game to the culprit," says Papa.

Papa wants us to keep this terrible thing to ourselves. He thinks that by our silence, the thieves might think their booty worthless. Mama wants us to keep our eyes open and look for clues as to who may have ransacked the wagon, like Western sheriffs do. I like Mama's idea best.

"Look at Grandma Bertie's beautiful hat!" calls Cori Jo. "Someone pulled it from the trunk and stepped on it with muddy shoes."

"Mama, will we be able to wash everything and get it to look like before?"

"It's impossible to get them washed and folded again while we're traveling, Emelie. They will just have to stay that way until we find a place to rest for several days."

As we travel on, the folks we're traveling with look different to me. I felt for a time we were all like family. Now I draw closer to my own for safety.

Grandma doesn't speak. Her silence fosters an anger in me towards those that caused her hardship. She turns over the wagon driving to me and she spends time alone inside the wagonr. As I sit and drive, I rack my brain to figure something out. Nothing comes.

When we stop to rest the horses, I sit with Grandma Bertie in the back of the wagon, among her trunks and boxes.

"You know, Grandma Bertie, I have some ideas on how we can capture the thief."

"Not now, my sweet Emelie, I'm still mourning my loss."

Days of travel pass with no sign of Grandma's belongings. Slowly she begins speaking. We talk about foiling the bandits at their own game. Perhaps by hiding behind a stand of trees in the dark of an evening. We'd keep the wagon open so the culprit would see there's no one around. Then, when he ventures into the wagon, we'd come out yelling and shouting like a pair of hyenas. Papa would hear us and with his gun he'd force the would-be bandit to his knees. Of course, we'd consider freeing him after he returned Grandma's possessions. Our imaginative stories seem to keep Grandma's spirits up.

When I'm alone, I try to figure out who the culprit might be. I go over every one of our wagon train families in my mind's eye. I've seen them plenty of times. Our noon stopping times are for socializing. I think of that young man I met. I wonder if his being so nice was a ruse. Finally I tell Stephen my idea.

"What are you thinking? You have no evidence," he says, and looks at me like I'm addled.

"We've got to begin somewhere."

"Maybe we can start by being alert, like Mama said. We can't act like we're suspicious and hang around watching what people do."

"I have a feeling about someone I've seen."

"Can you prove a wrongdoing?"

"I'm not sure. Will you help me?"

"Sure. Let me know what you want to do." Stephen leaves me to think about this by myself.

One beautiful summer morning two weeks after Grandma's loss, when the air is sweet with wildflower fragrance Bertie says to me, "Emelie, it's time to let my troubles just roll out onto the Trail. The worry about my box will have to take a back seat. We are in today, I have the best family all around me, and we're on our way to California. Why, that's a blessing right there!"

"Bertie, I knew you would say that one day. How nice that you picked today. On our noon break, let's celebrate. Please walk with me. We'll find nuts, leaves and berries left over from autumn. You can help me with their names."

We are no sooner walking when we hear a fight among two young boys.

"What happened?" I ask, going over to them.

"He knocked my berries on the ground."

"I didn't. Yer a liar!"

"You did. Yer the liar!"

A tear-stained face looks up at me and I don't want to lose this opportunity to practice my skills on the youngsters.

"I have an idea, boys. Grandma Bertie and I were just walking to find some berries. Come with us and we'll fill up your pails, as well as ours."

"I ain't going with him." The child runs away, leaving his pail of berries on the ground.

I look at Bertie, surprised at this response. She mouths an encouragement for me to continue.

"Would you like to walk with us to find more berries?" I ask the boy who was left.

Before he answers, we turn at a deep voice. It's the young man who helped me when I tripped. He's holding the hand of the youngster who ran from me just a few minutes ago.

"Here, Miss, someone wants to apologize to you," he says.

"Oh, thank you," I stammer. Then I squat down in front of my charge and say, "I'm sorry you ran away. I wanted to help you." I see some tears forming in his large brown eyes.

"I'm sorry I ran away when you were talking to me."

"I'm glad you came back. It makes me feel very angry when you run." I tousle his hair, hoping that will make a friend of him. "Here's your pail, there's room for lots more berries."

I watch the young boy dash away and think what a nice gesture it was for that young man to help. I hadn't known he was watching.

"Emelie, you are as good as a professional teacher," says Bertie. "And the young man who brought the child back to you seems to have the good sense that youngsters need to learn from. You might do well to speak to him about it sometime. There are many young children on this wagon train."

The clanging of the kettles sounds, and we all walk back to our wagons. I think about Bertie finding something good in that young man. That may make it even more difficult to prove my idea that he's the thief.

That night after dinner, we make a map to follow our travels. Papa gives us the *Guide*. We draw the Atlantic Ocean, New York, and Philadelphia on the right side. On the left we draw in the Oregon and California Territories near the Pacific Ocean. Further inland we sketch the Utah Territory and a big section known as "unorganized territory." Stephen's idea is to put circles where the cities of San Francisco and Sutter's Fort are. That's where we're headed.

Papa fills in the map with the forts and resting places. When I see vast spaces with nothing—nothing at all, I get the small and lonely feeling again. I clutch Aden's heart to help me feel close to something familiar. Soon as Papa is finished, I move into Grandma's wagon to write to Aden. There in the quiet, I can be as close to him in my mind as possible.

June 15, 1849

Dearest Aden,

Where should I begin? Grandma's box was stolen. It contained her valuables—jewelry and deeds relating to her land in California. She has been so calm in the face of this disaster. I doubt I would be.

Papa showed us his map tonight. I saw how rivers lead the way West and how the Trail follows them, looking like a mistake. Mistake I say because it meanders around and doesn't seem to take the shortest route.

We'll be stopping at military posts from now on because there are no more cities out here. Fort Kearny will be our first stop. Fur trappers go there to sell their pelts and replenish their stores. Next will be Fort Laramie. That is even more remote. Last of all, we'll stop at Fort Bridger, where Papa said the whiskey gushes forth like a waterfall. Mama looked disapprovingly when Papa said that, but he acted as if he didn't see her signal. Papa says it's a good thing the government keeps the forts operating, or we'd have a hard time traveling the 2,300 miles from Missouri to California without safe places to stop.

We have about 130 more days to travel.

I love you.

E

CHAPTER 12

Luck Comes to Our Wagon Train

Mid-June, 1849

This travel is not good for my brain. I cannot even keep the days of the week straight since leaving St. Joseph. Every day is either a weekday or a Sunday.

Today is Sunday. I smell it. Outside our wagons, Grandma Bertie is preparing Johnny cakes, bacon and stewed apples. Sunday breakfast always tastes better than other mornings. It's more leisurely and even Papa sits down with us. He's always got a prayer ready and there's no rushing to travel.

Things are very much the same since Grandma Bettie's box was stolen. There have been no clues. I've scrutinized the small boys of the wagon train, but they're too young to have thought of such an evil act. Sometimes I feel like the prairie is hiding the culprit like it hides the wagon ruts under the tall grasses.

When the afternoon is almost over and I'm about to take a long walk away from everyone, I see Sarah Robb, the midwife, walking towards our wagon carrying something. I walk over to meet her and find out she is carrying a cake for our family. Into our wagon we go and Mama cuts the cake immediately. I spread the oilcloth under the tree while Grandma makes tea. Sarah tells us the recipe and I write it down. What a surprise to find that it is made without milk or eggs.

"This is a good time for me to tell you of an impending birth. Maria Smith's time is drawing near. Can I count on both you Louisa and Bertie to help? I believe she'll be comforted knowing that you both are with her."

"It's good luck for our wagon train to have a baby born!" says Mama, happily. "Of course Bertie and I will do what we can."

"Since when do babies bring good luck?" I ask. "Aren't they a heap of trouble?"

"The good luck is that the hardships of life are forgotten when there's a baby to care for. You'll see, Emelie," says Sarah. "And, we can use your help, too."

"My help?"

"Of course. Your first job will be to tell others the news of the birth! You can even begin by clanging our kettle soon as we know," Sarah says in her friendly way.

I am disappointed despite Sarah's obvious belief that the announcement of the birth is as important as anything else.

A few days later, Maria is ready to give birth. Mama, Grandma Bertie, and I hurry to Maria's wagon. Despite Cora Jo's disappointment, Mama dismisses her from the excitement of Maria's wagon. She pouts as she goes to join David and some other children. A grown-up feeling comes over me and I begin to be in awe of what I may witness.

Sarah welcomes us in a quiet voice, and sends me immediately to heat water and fetch clean cloths from her wagon. This is what I like! They do need me. I go like a whirlwind. The rear canvas is open when I return. Maria is quiet. She is lying on quilts with her husband sitting by her side. As he holds her hand, his other hand smoothes her hair back away from her face. Such an intimate moment fills me with embarrassment. I turn away and look for Mama and Sarah, the cloths still in my hand.

They are all standing, quietly near the wagon, waiting.

"What's happening?" I whisper to Mama.

"The baby is waiting for the right time before he or she ventures into this world. Waiting is what we'll have to do, too."

"Sarah, do you think a cup of tea would help?" asks Grandma Bertie.

"Yes, the warmth might relax her."

"Emelie, would you fetch some tea for this soon-to-be Mama? And, while you're at it, bring some tea for us all," whispers Grandma.

I return with tea for everyone. I hear Maria groan and when I peek inside, I see her holding her swollen belly. Sometimes she cries out, and other times she's silent.

Grandma Bertie goes inside and sits on the other side of Maria. She lifts Maria's head and whispers for her to take a sip. Maria sips slowly. One sip after another.

"It won't be long now, my dear Maria. You'll see," Bertie says, looking comforted. She puts Maria's empty cup down and holds her own cup in her two hands and sips. I notice her nails are not as well groomed as they once were.

When Maria's cries come closer together, I feel the anticipation. Sarah asks Mark to leave the wagon. He gently kisses his wife's forehead and climbs out. He's been sweating. It must be hard work for him, too.

Now there doesn't seem to be any space between Maria's pains. Her breaths and cries are occurring in a rhythm. With each breath she seems to be in agony. This is not ever what I want to do. Did Mama go through this four times?

Sarah puts her hands on Maria's protruding belly and gently massages with downward strokes. She does this over and over. Now and then she peers between Maria's legs. I wonder how long this can last before the baby comes. I'm becoming restless. I look at Grandma Bertie, Mama and Sarah. They seem to be content with the way things are. I get up and stand at the back of the wagon. The sun is low in the sky and the men have begun the campfire. There was no traveling today because of Maria and her baby. For sure we'll be on the trail tomorrow with a new baby, the luck, as Mama calls it.

Cora Jo comes by the wagon.

"Want some food, Emelie? I can get some for everyone in the wagon." Then she peeks inside, "It hurts Maria, doesn't it?"

"Yes, but the baby is worth it," I say, trying my best to sound like Mama.

Mama looks up and shakes her head quietly, meaning no food yet. No one else looks up at me. I go back to Cora Jo and shake my head "no". She dashes away and I watch her legs catch her skirt. She slows to bunch the fabric in one hand to free her legs. Funny the way we wear skirts and the men don't. Someday I must speak to Mama about that.

I see the stars twinkling above the trees. My stomach is grumbling in emptiness, but I won't give up my position. It would be peaceful if Maria wasn't moaning in pain. Perhaps if there were no pain, there would be no luck.

Sarah calls, "I see the baby's head." My heart is beating like a hummingbird's wings. I don't know where to place myself, so I just stay close to the flap and watch the entire event. Sarah pulls the baby from Maria. The baby, who I see is a boy, is covered with his mother's blood, and for a moment I think I'm going to be sick.

Sarah cuts the cord that separates him from his Mama and he gasps for air, letting out a loud wail for such a little one.

That sound gives Mama and Grandma Bertie the signal to hug and laugh and tell Maria what a good job she has done. As they proceed to wipe the blood from mother and son, I remember my job. I jump from the wagon to clang the kettle announcing the little one's birth.

Now that I've witnessed his birth, I want to do something for him. Each day I find a place where the water runs clear and swift and wash the soiled diapers. I think about how nice little Adam will feel in them, and it doesn't bother me at all.

June 30, 1849

Dearest Aden,

A baby was born on our wagon train. I hold him a lot so his Mama can rest. It's at those times that I feel peaceful and forget where we are and where we're going. I'm careful not to breathe on his face. I wouldn't want to be the cause of his becoming ill.

The happy talk around here is that the tea Grandma gave to Maria helped to bring Adam into the world. Mama said a birth brings good luck. I'm waiting. I'd like it to be that we find the thief and Grandma's valuables quickly.

Love,
E

CHAPTER 13

Fort Kearny

Early July, 1849

The routine stays. I sit with Grandma Bertie whenever I can through days of the jolting, creaking, always moving wagon. Endless days, all alike, under a big open sky. Today was our turn at the back of the line. We endured the clouds of bugs and dust stirred up by all the wagons ahead of us. When we finally stopped for the noon meal, I dashed over to little Adam's wagon. He is the one diversion I have on this long, monotonous journey.

One day the Platte River's banks come into view. They look like huge snow heaps. My brothers are surprised to find sand dunes this far from an ocean. Nothing surprises me much anymore, so I put it in my memory box of all the things we've encountered so far. Mama is disappointed to see the wide but shallow Platte River. The turbid water means no one can drink—not even the animals. Surprisingly, it nourishes large blades of fresh, green grass. That's where our oxen will get their moisture. Horses need fresh water like we do—so we continue to search for springs each evening when we stop.

When we finally see Fort Kearny rising from the plains, we give a hoot and a holler! Adobe buildings glare in bleached whiteness that makes me squint. The entry gate is built from wood and has a sentry post high on top. But what's this? An entire Indian village encamped outside the gate to the fort?

Papa assuages my fear. "These are Pawnee and they help keep the Fort supplied with food and clothing, so the Army allows them to camp here," Papa explains. "It's all in this book," and he holds up the *Emigrants Guide*.

"No chance of attack, then?" Stephen asks.

"No, they wouldn't have the stamina. They've been fighting with the Sioux and dying from outbreaks of smallpox. Besides, they are not a fighting tribe."

Their teepees look like giant cones with smoke rising from the middle. All around the camp, children are playing just like our tykes do, chasing, laughing, and shouting.

Our wagon train stops near the Pawnee. Our children watch the others frolic and I can tell they want to join in, but don't. Not good to mingle with Indians, they've been told.

"Look at the H-frame! What a funny wagon. Is that a dog pulling it?" I ask.

"That's a travois," answers Papa. "It does the job when there aren't any wheels. See how the load is distributed? It's no hardship for a dog to pull."

Stephen looks at it carefully, inspecting the load.

"We could make one of these if we need to," he says.

"Do you think we may have to?" I ask, looking at Papa and Stephen.

"Never can tell. We're not half way to California, and already our horses are showing signs of wear," Papa says solemnly.

"What can we do?" I ask.

"Not use them," Stephen says, looking serious like Papa. "It's the stones and rocks that are hurting them. The gullies and sloughs that build up after a rain causes them to slip and strain their legs. The best thing is to get where we're going as quickly as we can," he answers, shaking his head the same as Papa does when he's worried.

Once we are inside the fort, gaiety overtakes me and I push Papa's words to the back of my brain. Stores selling clothes, food and trinkets and a Post Office fill the area nearest the entry. The Post Office is still the most popular stop after the commissary. It holds the mail for those who have a permanent address nearby yet live away from the route of the pony express rider. I love to look at the postage stamps required to be put on a letter before it can be sent. The photos on the stamps are not very good, but one can see the likenesses of Benjamin Franklin and George Washington. I'm amazed that all I have to pay is 10 cents. Sometimes I wonder if Aden has received any of my letters. Mama has written several letters to Nonna, but because we don't yet have a return address, we'll never know if our letters have been received.

We shop, return to clean our wagons and shop again. Our wagons will be bulging by the time we leave. All this shopping means we're a very long way from the next fort. I am enjoying the familiar faces in this unfamiliar place. It's all I need. I see Adam and his parents, Sarah, her husband and children, and the young man who helped me with the boys and the berries. His parents rarely accompany him, but I notice he walks with a purpose and finally disappears inside the commissary.

The dresses of the Indian women seem to be made of leather and they are short, only to the knees. The light beige color seems to complement their skin and hair, and I do believe I've never seen anything so pretty in the way of vestments on this trip.

"Mama, I'd love to have a short skirt like the Indian women have. They are a sight more practical than all this cloth swishing around our ankles." I grab my skirt for emphasis and hold up all the extra fabric that I have decided is quite unnecessary.

"Absolutely not. After this fort, we'll have no privacy when we relieve ourselves. There won't be a bush or a tree on the prairie to hide behind. Have you noticed how the skirts of our traveling women hide us? Native dress does not provide that." Mama spoke firmly.

"How do the Indians get their privacy?" I ask, really wanting to know.

"Enough of that," Mama scolds. So I decide to drop that subject for now.

Many families in our wagon train decide to eat inside the fort that evening rather than cook over a campfire. What a treat for us all!

There is only one restaurant serving food, and I hear the strains of music coming from inside.

"Papa, I bet the food here will be strange Indian food," I say, as we walk inside.

"Probably. But, I have a hunch they will not taste too strange to a hungry stomach."

"Bison," Stephen says. "I know they'll be serving that."

"I'm sick of fish, so I'm ready for anything," David chimes in.

We find there is no choice. It's bison stew, cornbread, or nothing.

The stew is delicious and I watch my family enjoying this time away from the strain of travel. What a treat to eat when someone else does the preparing, and the cleaning up.

Supper is punctuated by happy music: *Turkey in the Straw, Jimmy Crack Corn, Home Sweet Home.* My family and I drift over to watch the music makers after supper is cleared away. Papa takes Mama's hands and whirls her away on a dance floor about as big as our wagon's floor. I love to see her laugh. That young man comes over to Bertie and asks her to dance with him. I hear her complain about the creakiness of her joints, but our dear Bertie joins him, laughing gaily at her predicament. When the music stops, I walk around, enjoying this place as much as I've enjoyed anything. I still want Aden to be with me, but I fear I'm getting used to his absence. What will become of the two of us, I wonder.

I feel a tap on my shoulder. It's HIM! He motions to the music makers and nods his head with a questioning look in his eyes. Before any word comes out, he takes my hand

and has me dancing in the middle with the others. It is the most fun I've had since being on this journey.

"Thank you," I say to him when the music stops.

"Thank you," he says with a smile, and is about to walk away when I get up my courage to continue this conversation.

"I've been meaning to thank you for helping me with the young lad and the berries. I did need to hear him apologize or I would have lost faith in today's youngsters."

"I watched. I thought he needed to think about what he done."

"My name is Emelie. What's yours?" I hear my words and cannot believe I am so bold. It must be this wagon train that has changed me for good.

"Lawrence."

"Are you traveling all the way West?"

"Yes, with mammy and pappy."

That's it. Now I'm lost for words. "See you around," I say, suddenly becoming shy. I walk back to my family at our table.

By their conversation and smiles, I see Papa, Mama and Bertie still enjoying the moments of the dance.

"Wooo, Emelie! So you've taken up dancing with thieves, eh?" whispers Stephen in my ear.

"Listen, now I have a chance to find out what he is really like—and if he did it. Now, don't you go blabbing. He is still my best suspect."

As we walk back outside the Fort to our wagons, I'm aware of the sounds of the prairie night. A coyote howling, prairie dogs yipping and yelping, crickets singing in the dark. The sky is sparkling with stars, and for the first time in a long time I feel a peace at being here.

CHAPTER 14

Stampede

July, 1849

The next morning, yesterday's peacefulness gives way to confusion as our wagon train packs up for the next part of the journey.

"The good news from here on out is that we only have fifteen days of travel before we're at Ash Hollow. We've got a good river to guide us and, Louisa, good water, succulent grasses, and plenty of wood for fire are there. So, let's get a move on," Papa says.

"Looks like we're in for some wet weather," Bertie adds, as she points to our cone all tightly closed up. I see the cone is doing its job. Clouds, white, gray and black are gathering above us.

"Let's pull out before the rain hits us," Papa says.

"Gene, Emelie is going to try her hand at sharing the driving with Grandma. You think she's ready, don't you?" asks Mama.

"She's done a good job of learning with you, so I know she's ready. When's my Cora Jo going to get her chance?" Papa's question elicits a smile from Mama.

"Soon as we leave," Mama answers. "With the boys on the horses, it's up to the women and girls to keep our supplies moving."

The rain comes with hail and chills us to the bone. It follows us for four days before it stops. Everyone is working on drying out when a thunder-like noise stops us all. I am reminded of that rainy day the Natives surrounded us. The sound of their horses' hooves, muted in the soggy ground, was barely audible. But this is more. This is vibration, too. Our horses whinny, and they try to twist and jerk out of their harnesses. When the scouts' voices are heard over the bedlam of the animals and the clanging of the kettles, it's the dreaded word "Stampede!" they're shouting at us.

"Stampede? What's going on?" I ask Grandma Bertie. "What animals are stampeding? Horses? Cattle? Pigs?"

I see Papa ride up to Cora Jo and Mama in the wagon. "Hold tight to the oxen for they'll want to run!" He's shouting so loudly that Bertie and I in our wagon hear him, too. He rides over to us. "Bertie! Emelie! The boys and I are going to unhitch the mules from the back of our wagons and attach them to Josie and Brown. That may keep them from joining the stampede. Use good judgment. Be careful."

"Papa, what animals are stampeding?" I call out, but Papa is gone like the wind to the front of the wagon train.

"Bertie, will we be safe?"

"Frightened animals run wild. We'll be safe unless we can't hold onto our oxen."

I decide to slip down and whisper in Zebu's ear like I see Cora Jo do with Aurochs. I pat him on the head. It isn't long before I find myself patting less and slapping more as both oxen begin to shift and snort. They are lumbering to rid themselves of their yokes and begin their run. Zebu's great body is heaving and his head is moving up and down. The rope that holds them both looks strong enough and the wood of the yoke is fairly new, so we should be okay.

"Emelie, darling, you'd best come back here. Come on, now. Jump up with me," Bertie is shouting.

I scramble away from the fretful duo back onto the driver's bench. The noise around me becomes a roar. The oxen have come to life like I've never seen before. They are impossible to restrain, and my fingers are getting numb from grasping the leather strap. Our wagon begins moving fast. Grandma and I hold the reins together.

"We're not slowing them down, but they're still under yoke," Grandma calls out to me. I nod, but Grandma isn't looking. Her eyes bore straight ahead into the bedlam.

"Can you see Mama's wagon?"

"No, child. It's hard to tell where any of the wagons are now. It seems like we are all holding on for dear life."

Mud is raining down on us. Grandma and I are losing more control over the oxen every moment. My fingers are white where the reins have cut off my blood. I glance down at Grandma Bertie's and see red blood running down her hand.

"Grandma, your hand . . . there's blood!"

"No matter, child, we must keep to the reins. We all have more blood than we need, anyway."

Now we each have one hand holding the reins and the other holding us fast to the bench. Where is the Trail? I see wagons pulled off between bushes and rocks and their passengers holding on for dear life. The noise is terrible, worse than the loudest rumble of thunder. My insides are shaking so, I feel my skin will split open and they will fall out.

It's raining mud all around. The tall grasses hid the water before this. Now, as the grasses are being trampled down, the water is on top. We are flying through a lake of mud.

"I don't think I can hold on much longer, Grandma! My fingers hurt."

"Precious, we will hold on. We'll show them we're in charge. Don't even think of being frightened! We need all our strength to hold on. And, we're doing just that. Together we're doing just that!"

Grandma Bertie shouts. Her voice cracks from the strain. She coughs. I look at her hand again. Blood is flowing, but she's still holding on. I always knew she was not frail and delicate. For a moment I think I'm going to be sick to my stomach. I bend over, my head near my lap, and as I empty my stomach, Grandma Bertie's words remain in my mind.

We bump along from rut to rut, not speaking. It's too hard to be heard over the clamorous sounds. I notice Zebu is showing a pronounced limp. I elbow Bertie and jut out my chin towards the ox. Grandma acknowledges me with a nod. Then, right before our eyes, Zebu falls! The forward movement of the front wheels of our wagon continue until one wheel rolls partly over the great ox's body pinning him down and causing our wagon to tilt upward. Everything rolls back. Gaur continues tugging but she can't budge the wagon. She snorts and pants, but the wheel is stuck on Zebu. Grandma and I watch, stunned.

"Oh, we need help," I say.

"No, not yet," she reassures. "There's too much going on around us. We can't allow ourselves to be run over by other wagons and animals. Gaur will stop her struggling soon. She's going to tire. Then we'll have time for Zebu."

We sit, huddled together, arms tightly entwined while Gaur continues her struggle. It's hard to sit in the driver's bench at this angle. We haven't seen the stampeding animals with our eyes, but the terror of the commotion frightened us. I close my eyes and put my head on Grandma Bertie's shoulder for comfort. She pats my arm. I feel better.

Finally, the frenzy around us lessens. Human sounds become more audible. Children are crying, women wailing, men shouting. Gaur finally stops. She bends her knees to lie down but she is still yoked to Zebu. When she finally settles down, she is half on Zebu and half in the mud.

"We survived our first stampede!" Grandma Bertie says excitedly, hoarse from shouting, and laughing with tears streaming from her bright eyes. "We did it together, precious, you and me!"

We hug each other, a tight, tight hug.

"We've lost Zebu," she whispers to me.

"I know," I say. We keep hugging for a long time.

Then, remembering her hand, I take it in my own, turn it over and see the raw spot where the flesh had been rubbed away. Before Grandma can say "not yet," I go back into the wagon to find the water canteens. What a mess it is!

"Here, Grandma, drink some water, then I'll wash your hand. Relax and I'll have it cleaned quick as a wink."

I knew that hearing her own favorite phrases come from my mouth would make her laugh.

"Seems like I taught you something, didn't I? Soon you'll be sounding like we are family from way back."

She sips some water and closes her eyes to rest.

I take Grandma's hand and gently hold it out to the side. I pour water slowly in a stream over the wound until it is bright red without a speck of dirt covering it. Looking at her broken nails, I wonder at the energy inside this dear person that brought her into this wagon trail life. Her nails will need much more than water to rid them of the dirt that's part of them now.

"Now where could our family be? We'll be worrying till we see them again," Grandma Bertie says as she looks around. "I think it's safe to check on our poor beasts of burden."

I descend from the wagon with wobbly legs and a hurting head. Zebu's head is turned from his body in a strange position. The long eyebrows are still, the eyes unseeing.

"There's no breathing here," says Bertie mournfully.

"What will we do? We need two oxen to pull the wagon!" My tears feel hot on my cheeks, and when they get to my mouth I taste mud.

"It's time for another hug," she says. I get a hug from her, a firm, warm, loving hug, which I need badly.

"Let's go see if we can help Gaur. She's the needy one." Bertie holds on to me as we move towards the ox.

Gaur looks up at us, panting. Her large brown eyes look mournful and her lashes are heavy with mud. She looks so huge and helpless on the ground.

"Water. She probably needs water. Will you get our canteens, Emelie? I'll try to pour it right into her mouth so we'll not waste a drop."

Bertie speaks gently to Gaur. She wets her hand, and rubs it over her lips and into her mouth. When she begins to lap, I hold her mouth open. I see Gaur's thick tongue. Why, there's mud in her mouth, too. I wipe as much off with my fingers as I can, then watch as Bertie pours slowly so the water trickles to the back of her mouth.

"Not too much, now," she says to the ox. "We don't know where the next water source is. Be patient."

Gaur will not stand up no matter how Bertie and I try.

"I didn't check her feet," Bertie says. "Her feet may be the problem."

"I should have thought of that after listening to Stephen at Fort Kearny."

"Dear Emelie, for such a young one, you have a lot on your mind. It's a wonder you remember anything."

When we look, we see Gaur's bloody hooves.

A gunshot pierces the quiet. I look at Grandma, frightened at what that might mean.

"An animal too hurt to be saved," Bertie says softly.

We stay there, amid the mud and muck with dead animals within eye distance as the evening slowly brings its darkness. We lie down in our slanted wagon, and when we find some comfort there, we sleep.

We hear Papa's familiar voice calling, "Emelie! Bertie!" It is morning when they find us. Oh joyful day, comes to my mind. We are blessed to be found.

Hugs from Papa are the comfort we needed. Stephen, more reserved, mutters to me, "Good to see you, Emelie." Just hearing his words brings out the love I have for my brother.

"How's everyone else?" asks Grandma Bertie, in her still perky voice.

"David was thrown to the ground when Goldie took off to follow the herd. He's okay, but Goldie is gone," Stephen answers. "Goldie is high strung, and we had switched horses shortly before the stampede started."

"If we're lucky, someone has caught her, being the good riding horse she is when she's calm. But, no lamenting now. We've got to see about Gaur, here." Papa and Stephen look her over.

"It's only her feet, everything else looks fine. Let's all give a shove to get her standing again. We can wrap her feet with something before she walks again."

"Let me find a bandage of sorts," Grandma chimes in. She goes back into the mess that is in the wagon and comes out with two leather pouches. "We can wrap her feet in these after we use some equine grease."

"These pouches are handy between blacksmiths," says Papa. He smiles, "Bertie, what would we do without you and your remedies?"

"I hope you won't have to," she says.

I watch Papa bend down to examine Zebu. The four of us lift the wheel from her great body. I don't want to hear what is going to happen next. I slip inside the wagon and try to arrange things like they had been before the stampede. I want everything to be like before.

When Papa calls me to join them, I leave my tidying. I know what he's going to say, but I wait for his words. He leans against the wagon like he has all day to explain, and in his deep resonant voice tells me what has to be done to Zebu.

I can't help my crying, and with Papa's strong arms around me, I weep until I feel free of the ordeal we had just gone through.

Grandma Bertie and I stand close together. We wrap our arms around each other's waist, getting as close as we can get while Papa and Stephen make the necessary cuts to the hide. They were both muddy when they got here, and now they have blood splatters all over them. It's not long before Zebu is neatly sectioned in two, her blood forming rivulets in this boggy prairie soil. Blood, sickness, injury, death. It is all around us. We never leave it behind.

The task done, we sit close together in front of a campfire and listen to Papa tell what happened. "A herd of bison started to stampede, and although they were out in the distance, probably 15 to 20 miles from our train, the sound was picked up by the train animals. Mama and Cora Jo stayed in the wagon. Aurochs and Anoa withstood the stampede fairly well. Only a wheel was broken. The entire train is now spread over a twenty-mile distance and you are near the end.

"What about baby Adam and his Mama and Papa, Maria and Mark? And Sarah and Luke Robb and their little ones?" I ask.

"Thank God, they seem to be fine. A few broken spokes here and there, but nothing major."

"The Rhyss family didn't make out so well," says Stephen.

I can tell by Stephen's look that it's not good news. I take a deep breath knowing it will take some of the sting away.

"The Rhyss' had the worst time of anyone in our train. Mrs. Rhyss was in the wagon with her daughter and granddaughter when the oxen began to pull away. The wagon lurched, and the little girl tumbled out. Her Mama was so distraught that she jumped out after her. Both were trampled to death. Mr. and Mrs. Rhyss and their son, Lawrence, watched the whole thing."

"Lawrence? The young man I danced with?"

"Seems they wanted a better life than coal mining, and now they've lost half of their family. I doubt they'll continue."

My breath stops. I was accusing him of a robbery, but dear God, I didn't mean him any harm. What a terrible burden for the family to carry. I must get to him before their wagon pulls away. Oh, sorrow! I shan't press him for a confession. Being sad is its own punishment.

Families are in an upheaval deciding whether to reverse their travels or continue on. Papa says that if they turn back here, they'd arrive back at Fort Kearny in less time than it would take to reach Fort Laramie which is still two hundred fifty miles away. Despite us having only one wagon to travel with, Papa says we are not turning back. Grandma Bertie's wagon will be left and we'll hitch Gaur to ours along with Aurochs and Anoa. The three oxen will pull together. We have not traveled even one-third of the Trail and so much has happened. I try to imagine fitting everything we have into one wagon.

"I'm going to leave my clothing," Bertie says firmly. "Yes, these clothes will be out of style anyway. I feel like a true emigrant, and what emigrant carries such fancy clothes on the Trail?"

Bertie's clothing and bed linens are in two trunks. Both will be left out here on the lonesome prairie. From Maisie we untie her cooking kettles and the small portable stove we brought but never used. We put those items inside her wagon. What a find it will be for some folks traveling west if they have an extra ox or horse to pull it.

"What clothing will you leave?" Mama asks Cora Jo and me. I had already culled down my wardrobe when I left New York.

"I'm down to two dresses in the trunk and one on myself, Mama. Don't you think we need at the very least, three changes?" I ask.

"What you're wearing and one more dress with an apron will be sufficient. That goes for Cora Jo, too. We're not going through big cities, it's wilderness from here on out."

"One to wear and one to spare," calls Grandma to us.

Cora Jo and I remove any extras we had with us. "One to wear and one to spare" keeps running through my brain. And they can be replaced. What the Rhyss family has left behind can never be replaced.

All the next day, Mama and Grandma dry the meat that was once Zebu. They begin at sunrise with a fire, and when the flames are low and smoking, they hang the strips of meat over lines that Papa and the boys had fashioned across our wagon to a tree and back again. The smaller the strips, the quicker the meat dries. I find Mama and Grandma checking the meat often, and even cutting some strips smaller and thinner than we had.

By the next morning, it is all jerked and we find we have much more than we need, so Mama, Grandma, and I visit the remaining wagons to give them a share. I ask Cora Jo to come along, but all she does is sob and remind us that she'll never eat meat again.

At the Rhyss wagon, I see the freshness of their tragedy everywhere I look. Mr. and Mrs. Rhyss and Lawrence have their sadness upon their faces, in their eyes that seem like puffy red slits, and in their bodies that are stooped like puppets whose strings are askew. Their arms and hands hang from their shoulders like weights instead of working appendages. I feel ashamed that I carried such malice in my thoughts. I deceived him into thinking I was friendly, when all the time I was testing him.

They thank us for the jerked bison. I tell them that it is chewy but tasty, and that I hope they'll like it. The Rhyss's remain like broken statues. I am terribly sorry for them. I look at Lawrence in his sorrow. I doubt that he is the one who took Grandma's box.

As I walk along the train, I see pots, pans, luggage and trunks placed on the ground. Some of the boxes are open with colorful clothing bulging out the top. Those folks were like Grandma Bertie, who planned to settle California in style. Little did they know what we now know. The beautiful wood and jade box won't be here in the discards, but I look anyway, as discreetly as I can.

CHAPTER 15

A Divided Wagon Train

July, 1849

"Papa, now that we have three oxen to do the same work two did, will we be making better time?"

"No, Emelie, oxen move only so fast, whether it's one hauling or fourteen."

"When do Milo and Maisy get to show us how valuable they are?"

"Be patient. The mules will get their turn."

In the evening, I ask Stephen to walk over to the Rhyss wagon with me.

"I've noticed that he and his family keep to themselves. I think if we're friendlier towards him, we may find out more about him and his family. Friends can't hide things from friends very well."

"You still think he's guilty? I can see that his family does not have much. Their wagon looks shabby and worn. That still doesn't seem like a reason to accuse him. Just because folks are poor doesn't mean they steal from others. Besides, Emelie, they've suffered a great tragedy. This is not the time to be playing detective."

We approach the Rhyss campsite. It is quiet. I hear someone working quietly. I look at Stephen. We walk further into the stand of cottonwoods and see Lawrence slitting branches of wood.

"How are you doing today?" I ask, timidly.

He smiles weakly at me, and nods his head. He looks back at his wood.

"What you got there?" Stephen asks.

"Faggot. Burns quickly when you slash it."

"Like kindling?"

"Yeah, only this faggot will light a special fire to banish evil spirits from our family, our wagon and the entire train." He doesn't look at us but keeps his eyes to the wood he's cutting. I notice the thin pieces of wood curl after they've been slashed.

Stephen and I look at each other. I think he must be daft.

"You from Kentucky?" I ask him.

"Yeah." Lawrence answers but still watches what he's doing.

"What brought your family this far?"

He slowly puts down his knife and the branch he was working with and looks at us. Somehow I feel like an intruder. I sit down on a grassy knoll and move my fingers over the blades of grass and twigs. We wait. After an eternity, he begins.

"First the coal mine was making me and Pap sick. Then Patrick, my brother-in-law was killed in a collapse. We took my sister and her baby in to help them out. We thought it would be best for all of us to begin anew. We scrimped and saved for this travel. And now, Margaret and Mary are gone forever."

"I'm so sorry for you and your family. Losing a sister and a niece at once is a lot to bear," I say, almost in a whisper. "Is there anything we can do for you?"

He looks so pathetic sitting there. I see his eyes filling up. I'm beginning to feel pity.

"No. The jerky was good and I thank you again for that. We're managing best we can. We figure it best to be away from this place."

"I understand," I say. "Does that mean you'll be turning back?"

"No, we'll go on. Nothing's back East for us anymore."

We watch quietly as his knife slashes the wood into thin pieces.

"Like to fish?" Stephen asks.

He nods, yes.

"Come fishing with us soon as we find a fishing creek further up the Trail, how's that."

"Look forward to it." Lawrence says, unsmiling, and looks back down at his curled wood strips.

Stephen and I know it's time to leave. We softly say 'bye, and quietly walk away.

"You know, Stephen, I actually had fun dancing with Lawrence at Ft. Kearny. I think he might have become my friend, but now with this loss, he'll probably stay to himself. It will be hard from here on out to find out more about him and the disappearance of Grandma's box."

"So what do you want to do next, Sheriff?"

I give my brother a look that should whither him, but all he does is laugh.

Several days later, Stephen and David find something to get the travelers in a tizzy—a buffalo bone with the word "Injuns" scratched on it. It's a rule of the Trail to leave information for those who come after, so Papa makes the boys return the bone to the place it was found, and then the kettles clang for a meeting.

The group gathers, and the Rhyss men are among them. Papa tells of the bone my brothers found.

"I know that some of you will want to change our routine. No resting at noon. Traveling as quickly as we can through this territory," Papa begins. "But our animals are wearing out. Just check their feet. They're bloody and their shoes are wearing out. It's going to hurt us in the long run if we don't rest them. Contending with Indians is a good sight better than being stranded here with no animals to pull us West. I propose we keep to our plan and rest during midday."

I hear grumbling among some, and agreement among other families. We wait. It is a hard decision.

A man whose name I don't know speaks, "Mr. Grandi, we care about the animals, but we care about our families, too." He looks around at everyone and nods for emphasis. Some others nod back in agreement. 'Work like a horse,' the saying goes. That's what they're supposed to do. I'm for changing the way we travel. I suggest we travel sunup to sundown—and get out of these plains as quickly as possible."

Some folks are nodding "yes." Mamas are holding on to their youngsters. No one looks happy.

"Sioux means scalping," calls another man. "We don't want Armageddon like in the Bible. It's bad enough the way it is without tempting the Indians with our presence."

Mr. Rhyss surprises us by speaking. "You got to realize that we are a travelin' folk and our critters are a travelin' with us. We get weary. We need rest. So do they. I'm going along with Mr. Grandi, here. I want to rest my oxen. Who wants to do the same?"

Before long, the folks are sorted into two groups: those who want to keep the nooning time for resting, and those who don't.

"Let's get to it, then," says Papa, loudly. I hear the anger in his voice. "Some of you folks can leave, while those who want to continue as we have, will do so. Good luck to both of us."

Folks move slowly towards their wagons. It seems like nobody really wants to separate, but that's what they're doing.

"Fright is a terrible thing," Mama says. "It makes strangers of folks who were once friends."

Sarah, Luke and their three children walk over to us. Soon Maria, Mark and little Adam join us, too.

"We're staying with you throughout this journey," says Sarah, giving Mama and Bertie a hug.

Maria walks near me. "You are so good with Adam, Emelie. Why, I know my little boy would miss you terribly if we were not together during this journey."

"Helping with little Adam is more fun than work. Really, it is." I'm embarrassed by her words. I reach for little Adam and give him a hug. He has a sweet smell about him, like babies often do.

"Wouldn't it be fine if we get to pass the others even though we rest at nooning each day? Then we'd be chiefs of the Trail!" exclaims David. A little parade of children commences chanting, "We're chiefs of the Trail!"

We all laugh. I feel better when I see the men relax. Papa makes me feel like we can conquer the whole of the West just by keeping the animals well.

I wonder with all this change if the robber will be moving on with the others where I cannot reach him.

One morning I see Lawrence at the creek fetching water for the day's trip ahead.

"I'm glad you're going along with us," I say, cordially.

"It didn't start off real good, but we've still got hope."

We're silent. I'm thinking of a way to turn the conversation around.

"Our Grandma Bertie had her own wagon when we started. She had raiments and baubles fit for a queen. It was a pity to see her leave everything behind because she lost an ox and had to give up her wagon. She rides with us now."

"Sorry about the ox." After some silence, Lawrence continues. "Why are you going west?" he asks.

"Gold, adventure, education."

"What about Miss Bertie?"

"Going to claim her land in California, land that is filled with gold."

"How does she know that, if she's never been?"

"She suspects it. There's a lot of gold out there."

"She's a brave Missus to travel so far."

"Yes."

"How does anyone know where one's land is? Everything is so spread out."

"Well, our Bertie knows. She has a deed to prove it."

"What's that?"

"A legal document that has measurements on it."

"We never owned anything 'cept the clothes on our backs. Pap's dream is to own some property. Mam had that dream, too."

"What do you plan on doing for work?"

"Pap and me got strong arms from the mines. Lumbering, fishing, we can do it all. Been working since age nine. I figure I know how."

I nod in agreement, get my buckets and turn to leave, feeling both sorrow for him and his folks and defeated in my lack of courage to bring up Bertie's missing box.

"See you later," I say.

"Your name means "excel," Emelie. I hope your excelin' shows as we travel on," he calls after me.

"What's your native language?" I ask, surprised that he knew my name.

"Celtic."

"I sure hope some magic light shines upon us and we all excel in this journey," I say. Several days later, we see Lawrence leading Goldie towards our wagon.

"Hey there," calls Stephen. "You found our horse?"

"Figured she was yours," Lawrence answers.

Papa comes out from behind the wagon. "Well, what do you know. That's Goldie, all right. A little worn and frazzled, but our horse, all right."

We all gather around the horse as she swishes her tail. Papa and Stephen run their hands over her body feeling for injuries and Cora Jo runs to get her a dried apple.

"She was in a meadow you can't see from here. I've watered her already, but she sure can use some brushing," Lawrence adds.

"I'll say," says Grandma Bertie. "Why, I almost wouldn't have recognized her. There now, Goldie. We never thought we'd see you again."

"Can I ride her first?" David asks.

"She can't take a rider until she feels safe again, David. Remember, she was as frightened as you," says Papa.

"Can we tie her to Oldie, since they both pulled Grandma Bertie's wagon before we got the oxen? Maybe she'll like that," adds my sister.

We've got Goldie back. I feel that maybe there is some kind of goodness following us after all. We've got our traveling group together: the Smiths, the Robbs, and the Rhysses. And although my bottom is beginning to hurt from the everlasting bumping of the hard wagon, Grandma doesn't complain and neither do I.

CHAPTER 16

Lawrence

July, 1849

Our travel days are measured by the stampede. On the tenth day after that terrible event, we see Indians! Campfires are cooking our suppers when the Natives appear. They are motionless as statues. Their brown bodies are shiny with sweat, their dark hair long and windblown. On their faces I see stripes of color. I notice their mouths are drawn up at the sides, as if they find us amusing. They seem to anticipate our meeting, as are we.

Sarah and Maria hold tightly to their children. Our men walk towards them and wait for some signal of friendship. The chief, who has more paint on his face than the others, walks towards us. He holds out his hand to Papa, who grasps it in a handshake. Then he holds out both his hands, and turns them over. Papa nods "yes" at that gesture. I think they'll leave as they came.

But, no! The chief waves his arm and like puppets, his men slip off their horses. They move quietly as they surround the wagons. In an eye blink, they jump into our wagons. We watch from outside the canvas cover. It doesn't take long before they become bolder. We watch, immobile, as they begin touching items: metal kettles, oilcloth, mattresses.

Sarah goes quickly into her wagon while Luke holds his tykes and stays to watch with the rest of us. One Indian finds the last jar of pickles in our wagon. He opens it and puts the jar to his lips. In a blink of an eye, he is spitting out and holding his throat. He places the jar over the fire, which promptly cracks and the pickles sizzle and hiss until they become ash. He backs away, his eyes not leaving the fire, to join the others. All the boys are stifling laughter, but I notice that Mama, Grandma and the other grown-ups remain stony-faced.

When their curiosity is satisfied, the Natives mount their horses and the chief again approaches Papa for a handshake. They all leave as quietly as they have come.

"That was a nice greeting," says Papa. "Let's hope their greetings will always be as pleasant."

Once they are gone, we stoke the campfire and sing in celebration. Thank goodness for Mark and Luke. It is nice to hear the guitar and banjo at a time like this. The melodies they play remind me of home. Home with Aden.

We talk around the campfire. Papa's *Guide* tells us that the Nebraska Indians are Cheyenne. Friendly Indians. We have nothing to fear. We agree we made the right decision way back when we separated from the others. It fills me with a feeling of safety.

I take to riding some each day. I love the wind in my face. It brings the scent of dry air with it. When my hair blows up off my neck, I'm cool as a soft rain showering over me, and, the bumping up and down on Josie's back never hurts my bottom like the wagon does. Lawrence has begun to ride when he sees me galloping along the caravan. We don't talk during those times, but I feel like I'm making headway into a friendship.

Our travel becomes routine and we get to the South Platte River easily. Our five wagons stop atop the high banks, reminding me of huge animals guarding the half-mile of water that has to be forded. The river itself looks like a thick braid. There is movement going in all directions. Hummocks are forming over brush. Eddies are swirling into whirlpools.

I look around the high land surrounding the river and see there is no timber to help us cross.

Lawrence goes down to the riverbank and feels the water.

"I'll swim to other side to test the depth and current." He splashes the cold water over his body. I see that the muscles in his arms are well developed. Coal mine work must take a lot of strength.

Lawrence ventures in, moving slowly toward the midstream current. With the next step he disappears!

"Close call," he yells to us, dripping wet and laughing at the way the hole took him by surprise. He moves ahead. "Here's a sand bar," he calls as he stands waist high in the water.

He continues on and I see him being pushed by the current. Every now and then he turns and waves to show us he's okay. Soon the rushing of the river makes his voice inaudible.

When he reaches the other side, we shout whoops of joy. He waves and then begins his return. We gather around as he describes the kind of trip we'll have across the South Platte with our wagons, oxen, horses and mules!

"We must cross in an arc or the wagons will surely overturn in the strong current. And we must keep moving. There's quicksand out there in spots."

"Thanks, Lawrence. We're ready now. We'll be first and everyone can learn from our mistakes," says Papa to the group.

"Mistakes? We can't have any of those!" says Mama.

"I always wanted to be a guinea pig!" twinkles Grandma.

"I'm ready to go again, this time helping out with the stock. Can you use my help?" asks Lawrence, moving up to where Papa is standing. Papa twirls the corner of his moustache, and then gives Lawrence a broad smile. That's Papa when he happy about something.

"Yes, I'd like that. How about you, Luke and Mark, taking the horses? My boys will untie our mules, Milo and Maisy, and walk them across. I'll walk with the oxen. All the women folk will ride the wagon."

"Let's go," calls Mama. She's eager to get this over with. "Let's sit on the floor of the wagon and hope it doesn't turn into a boat!"

I notice Lawrence rubbing Goldie and whispering in her ear. I bet he did that when she was lost, before he brought her back to us. He seems to know about animals even though his work was in a mine. And I wonder where he learned to swim. Mayhap there are rivers in Kentucky.

Lawrence leads Josie and Brown while Luke follows with Goldie and Oldie. Papa has a good hold on our oxen as we plunge into the river with words "Be careful! Good luck!" ringing in our ears.

"This is bumpier than land travel. Hold on, girls!" says Mama giggling.

"Mama, are you having fun?"

"Why, yes, Emelie. This is quite a bit different from our monotonous days on the Trail. How are you doing, Bertie?"

"I admit this is more enjoyable than I thought it would be."

Seeing Mama and Grandma happy helps me feel less frightened. Still I wish I didn't feel every push of the current and every pull of the oxen.

We make it without a mishap! Before we stretch out on the new bank, Lawrence and Luke are in the water again, returning to help the others cross. Looking across to the place we just left, I notice that everyone is out watching and waving except Sarah. She hasn't watched us cross? She must be frightened. Maybe if she doesn't see the dangers, she won't be so frightened when her time comes.

It takes most of the afternoon for all the wagons to cross. We make camp right where we are for the night. Mark Smith and Luke Robb provide the music again, and as we sing and laugh, we pretend to throw our troubles into the campfire.

The trek to Ash Hollow, our last rest before Fort Laramie, begins and ends without a mite of trouble.

"A little bit of heaven, that's what this Ash Hollow is!" exclaims Bertie. "With such water, shade trees, and grasses for the herd, could this be the California we've been seeking?"

"We've had our trials coming this far. I would welcome this as our destination," says Mama. She looks at Papa, who ignores her arched eyebrows waiting for an answer she'll like.

"Now please, ladies. We are only about 200 miles West of Fort Kearny. We're not even out of Nebraska yet!" Papa sounds exasperated. "We'll have time to rest when we get to where we're headed."

One day Stephen yells, "There's Courthouse Rock. It's not a mirage, either! It's the biggest thing around here."

I look in the direction of the giant mound. How strange it is, rising up like that. It looks like a mirage, all pink and brown and smooth.

"And I thought the sand dunes near the Platte were large. They look like ant hills next to this one," I say, happy we've come this far. "Papa told us we'd see Courthouse Rock. I do think folks become dolts with this incessant traveling. How can they call a lump of earth a courthouse? Honestly, Stephen, does this look like a courthouse to you?"

Soon the second landmark rises out of the prairie. We all see it and yell happily after we're certain it's not a mirage. A tall column, four hundred feet high, that actually looks like a chimney gives us another boundary in this vast openness. Its presence means we're only fifty miles to Fort Laramie. Two or three days at the most.

"Look at the different colored sand. All chocolate, white and tan around the chimney," calls David.

"What else is here?" asks Cora Jo, getting grumpier by the day.

"Water, good fresh water for us all," Mama answers.

The water is in a deep gulch. It's a bubbling spring with stones. David is right in the middle of it looking for stones to add to his collection.

I find Lawrence and ask him to walk around the limestone Chimney Rock with me. The golden glow from the setting sun changes the color of the limestone making it look like a mirage. We climb up a ways and look at the shadow the rock makes on the prairie below us. I wave my arms like a crazy bird and get him to laugh. That's the first time he's laughed so heartily.

"Look out there on the horizon. That's where we're going. Did you ever wonder how long it would take for us to get to the place where the earth and sky meet?"

"You never get there," says Lawrence. "It keeps moving off to another place."

"I know that. But just pretend if we could get there . . . it might make the trip go faster. We could travel from horizon to horizon."

"I don't pretend much, too much real stuff around to consider."

The silence becomes uncomfortable. So I start again.

"All that gold we're heading for. Probably no one bothers to steal from others, because so much is around for everyone," I say, hoping he catches my drift.

"I reckon they'll be crooks there like everywhere else."

"Guess you're right. Did you ever take something that wasn't yours?"

"No. I never saw anything I wanted bad enough to break a commandment."

"Not even here where the law is different?"

"Mam talked about God's commandment, not man's laws."

By now, the Robb children are chasing Cora Jo and David around the Chimney and we laugh at their antics. The spell is broken, but I'm thinking Lawrence isn't the thief. He's too, well, different.

CHAPTER 17

Mormon Ferry Crossing

Early August, 1849

We finally arrive at the Mormon Ferry Crossing. All kinds of wagons are surrounding the docking area, waiting their turn. I don't see the ferry, but I can see a small village nearby. The houses, built solidly to last, says Papa, line the narrow road. As we travel towards the docking area, I notice how well cared for they are. Gardens full of flowers, climbing and spilling over their boundaries, seem to welcome us. I'm looking forward to meeting these folks.

"One dollar and fifty cents!" Mama calls out. "They are charging a small fortune to cross the river."

"Now, Louisa, remember what we went through at the South Platte crossing? The North Platte is deeper here. It would be a bargain at twice the price," Papa answers. "The ferry was built for their own people who were traveling west to settle. They hadn't planned on other travelers looking for a way across. When they found it profitable to run the ferry for others, some settled here and never got further west at all."

Mama calms down when she sees our former caravan members in the crowd. We are greeted with hugs and pleasantries. I like this time, catching up on news since our separation. They hadn't run into Sioux Indians, but they've had other troubles since leaving us.

Many of them lost oxen and horses. Seems like they walked them to death. Some fell over and died on the spot. When they realized they were helpless without their pulling animals, the folks began walking—what else could they do? They'll be joining up with other wagon trains here. A few families toted the belongings of others in their wagons and were now waiting for new oxen to be walked in from Deseret. I'm glad there are no hard feelings between us. Camaraderie is a necessity so far from civilization.

When I see the ferry I am ready to scream. Of course I don't. It's a raft with a rope overhead spanning the width of the river. Two men get the ferry moving. One has a long pole and pushes from down deep in the river bed while the other pulls the overhead rope. Primitive travel that I'd better get used to.

Like all our river crossings, it's one wagon at a time. Papa figures we'll have a long wait. When Mama hears this, she decides to move away from the bedlam of the docks.

"Let's go wandering around this village, ladies. Eugene, you and the men can wait in line," she says.

"Mama, this surely is one of your best ideas!" I say.

We stroll past the gardens. Grandma Bertie's sharp eye points out the blooming herbs mixed in with the flowers. Everything is colorful and fragrant. Backyard farms are growing vegetables. The change of scenery even calms my grumpy sister.

"These folks have turned the dust of the high prairie into fertile land. They must be very inventive people," says Mama.

A woman sweeping smooth the hard-packed dirt of her front yard looks up at us. Feeling a new braveness, I call out "Hello," and she answers with a smile.

"Is there anywhere to eat in town? We're all hungry and are willing to pay," asks Mama.

"For how many?"

"Twenty-two. We are somewhat tired of beans and jerky. Fresh vegetables would be a treat."

The woman stops her sweeping and looks us over. A bonnet shades her head but the strings hang loose and blow freely in the breeze. Her apron has a large pocket filled with something heavy. "I gather you are waiting your turn at the ferry," she says. "I can feed you, but I cannot seat all of you at one time. If you come in two groups, the first around five this afternoon, I'll have a meal for you."

"Why, thank you. I did not expect such kindness," says Mama. The woman returns Mama's smile and watches us continue our walk.

"We have the first group right here," Bertie says. "After we eat, we can keep our place in line while the men and boys have their turn."

"Bertie, could we do it in reverse? Could we be the last ones to eat? Is that okay with everyone?" I ask, looking about for approval.

"Not hungry, Emelie?" Mama asks.

"No, it's not that . . ." I answer, not wanting to say more.

"That's fine with me," Grandma says. "Let's go tell the men."

I like it here. The order is pleasing. Everything seems exact and well planned. This is what I need to catch my thief. I turn around to wave at the sweeping woman. She's now sitting on a bench in the midst of her flower garden, reading. She is lost in the pages and doesn't acknowledge us any longer.

Bertie and I catch each other's eye at the sight of her. "I imagine it's a Bible," she whispers to me.

"I've heard they're religious people," I answer, nodding my head.

"I'm not particularly hungry," says Sarah, as the rest of us prepare to walk back to the woman's house for the evening meal. "And I don't mind jerky and beans. My stomach probably wouldn't take kindly to real fresh food!"

"Jiminy, Sarah. You don't want some good food to eat for a change? Can we take Kate and Daniel with us? And, do you think Lily will come, too? That would give you a well-deserved break."

"Yes, you can have all my little ones!" Then she looks at her tykes and says, "Would you like that? You can pretend you are in Cora Jo's and Emelie's family tonight."

The children look up shyly at us, but they cling close to their Mama. How funny they are. One minute they are begging to stay with us, and the next they look so shy!

The dinner is served after an extensive blessing. And I always thought Papa's were long. I glance at the children of the family who are sitting on one side of the long table. They keep to their eating and don't look over at me. They must be comfortable eating with strangers. They clear the plates when the last one is finished. I rise from the table to do my share, and although I am asked to remain seated, I want so much to learn about these folks that I continue to pick up the utensils and plates that are near me.

In the kitchen, I almost beg to help, and reluctantly, the oldest girl, who has begun to wash the plates, allows me to dry them.

"When Mama comes in, you'll have to stop," she tells me. "She doesn't like strangers in our kitchen."

"Do you do feed strangers often?" I ask, careful to pick up and dry one plate at a time.

"Oh, yes. People pay us, then we can buy what we need." She doesn't look at me, so I watch the steam come from the basin of hot water she's using.

"We're not Mormons." I put a plate down on a fresh white tablecloth.

"Yes. We can tell."

"How's that?" I take another plate. My ears are perked up because her voice is very soft.

"It's little things that give you away."

"What things?" I'm drying quickly because I'm feeling betrayed. I don't like it when folks think they know me because of the way I look.

"You don't work all the time like we do."

"We do work, but we aren't working now because we're waiting for the ferry."

"Do you have animals? Do you have needlework? Do you have woodworking tools? Do you have books? Do you have pen and paper? We would be working with these things all the time, even while traveling. Idle hands are devil's hands."

"I never thought of it that way." I'm dumbstruck by the way she rattled off.

"And your hair. It's unbound."

"My hair?"

"Your brother, he spoke with a full mouth."

"Ummm" is about all I can manage. I feel like dropping a plate on the floor to interrupt her orderly life. She is about to scold again when I drop it, and the shattering noise brings her mother into the kitchen. She politely asks me to leave. I can tell she doesn't want her daughter speaking with me. I apologize for the broken plate; thank her for the delicious food, curtsy, and hurry to join the others.

I'm angry with everyone in this village because of her. Who does she think she is, telling me that we look lazy? I bet she wouldn't have survived the journey we're taking. I was curious about these folks. Now I know they're nervy and rude, too. I can't wait to leave. Ferry or no ferry, I'd just as soon swim the river than see the likes of her again.

The others have begun their short walk to the docks. I keep them in sight, but purposely walk slower so I can think about what she said: "It's the little things that give you away."

CHAPTER 18

Latter Day Saints

August, 1849

The ferry ride doesn't come soon enough for me, and when Papa suggests that we be last, I'm cross as a bear. I don't need to spend any more time in this horrible place.

Luke Robb has the little ones around him watching the activity. When their turn comes they squeal like piglets seeing their slop. Where is Sarah? Frightened as she was at the South Platte River crossing?

Our turn finally comes at dusk. "See you down the Trail!" we call out to those behind us, and then hang on to our few items as we are pushed away from the dock into still another land.

We are away from the green of Deseret, and the landscape seems bleak. Dry prairie soil is kicked up by the oxen. Grandma suggests we wear bandanas over our noses to stop us from sneezing. Now that there's no river to follow, the monotony of the Trail makes me groggy. I miss the Platte and the changes it brought. However the water flowed, bubbling or quiet, animals always came.

We haven't been permitted to drink river water since Tim's death. When we find springs where water oozes from a wall of rocks, we indulge ourselves. Otherwise we boil water, which is more work than I like. Sometimes I think Mama is overly cautious. I doubt Western rivers have the cholera disease floating around like the Ohio did. "Better to be safe than sorry," I hear Bertie say, and we dutifully boil away.

One day, in the shadow of Independence Rock, I take the Robb children for a walk. Lily is lagging behind, but I know the walk is good for her. I rest a moment to watch the others in front of me. When I turn around to check on Lily, I see her put a piece of dried buffalo dung in her mouth.

"No! No! Buffalo droppings," I scold, nearly scaring her speechless. Keeping her safe has gotten to be one of my jobs. At least it gives me something to do. Little Adam and his Mama have grown stronger, and I am no longer needed to do daily chores for them. I've been giving Sarah and Luke some peace of mind by taking their little ones on outings when we stop. I put Lily in my arms and continue walking hoping to leave the dung way behind.

"Looky here!" I shout to everyone. My brothers and sister come running.

In front of me is a mound of quilts and bedding. Over there are guns. Wagon wheels make another pile. I put Lily down and take her hand, and we dash along from one pile to another, laughing. She thinks it's a game. As we turn around a bend of the Rock, we stop short. Two men, one gray bearded and tall, the other somewhat pudgy, are scavenging the items. They look up at our commotion.

"Hello, there. Do any of these belong to you?" one of them asks, as he waves his hand over piles of items.

"No," I answer, surprised at finding such a cache here, and even more than that, others who are patiently looking through it all.

"We'll continue then."

I stand there perplexed and watch them pick up each item, look it over carefully, and then form other piles.

"What are you going to do with all these things?" Stephen asks.

"We take the ones we can clean and repair. They're like new when we finish, then we sell them," the tall one answers, still looking things over.

"To whom?"

"Anyone who needs them."

"Where'd all this come from?" Stephen asks.

"Folks leave them. The traveling is rough all the way down to Deseret on the Great Salt Lake. Lightening their wagons makes it easier."

"Are you Mormons?" I ask.

"We prefer the name 'Latter Day Saints,' he responds, as he continues working.

"Do you mind if we look over the items?"

"No, go ahead. There are some good things here, you'll see."

"Let's find something," I say to the children, and we proceed to look over one pile then another.

"Emelie, come here. I like this!" Kate calls.

"Kate, that's a feather bed you found. Lucky you. Come on Lily and Daniel. Let's go see what Kate found."

The children roll about on the mattress, giggling and shouting to each other. They pull up the ends and hide in the folds. They pretend the feathers are water and jump into them. I'm laughing along with them when Lawrence comes to sit by me.

"Find anything you like?"

"We've too much already, but these tykes are having fun, ain't they?"

"'Aren't they' is what you must say."

"Okay, I'll say it, but it don't slide out like 'ain't' does."

"Oh, Lawrence, you'll learn," I giggle. "It will just take time."

"Hello there! What's going on?" Luke calls.

"Papa, look what we've found," calls Daniel.

"Mr. Luke, I'm so glad you've come," I say. Just look at all this, and there are your little ones, having the time of their lives on that feather bed!"

"Are the other folks on their way, too?" asks Lawrence.

"No, they got too used to sitting without bumping along, to walk over." Luke answers.

"Look down there," I point to the group. Latter Day Saints are scavenging items that can be repaired. My brothers are with the others, watching. Kate found the feather bed among the items that were left as folks lighten their wagons. She's having such fun with it."

"Say, maybe I'd better look for some musical instruments. I've got to get you two a'playing to help out Mark and me."

"You'll be wasting your time on me, Mr. Luke. Mama made me play piano but nothing stuck."

"Had a whistle I carved out myself. That's about it for me," says Lawrence.

"We'll see about that, I'm going to take a look. If I'm lucky, you'll both be playing sooner than you think."

"Kate, Daniel, Lily, come. Let's go with your Papa to look for something that makes music."

We all follow Luke down to the piles.

"What's this here? A banjo?"

"Strings are broke," Lawrence says as he looks it over. "Can fix those in a jiffy."

"Look here. A melodeon. Probably too heavy for the owners to carry. How about taking it back? One of our wagons must have some room—it's special for sure."

"Yes, Papa. Let's take it and the feather bed. I must have the feather bed," says Kate.

"Okay, my sweetie. Jump up and we'll look out over yonder. See where our wagon train is? You'll have to do your share of hauling. Think you can manage?"

Lawrence and I catch each other's eye and smile at the thought of little Kate dragging the feather bed behind her. Luke asks the Saints about their work, gets permission to cart off the items he wants, and we all start back. The boys carry the melodeon, Lawrence and I lug the feather bed, and Luke walks with his children.

"Christmas in August," yell the boys as we approach. Before long, everyone is out looking over our treasures.

"Luke Robb, we are trying to rid ourselves of extras, and here you go and bring more home. Oh, my. What a husband I have. He's sure to build me a big house so he can keep all his 'finds' in it!" Sarah says.

"After dinner, Lawrence and Emelie will get their first music lesson," reminds Luke.

"Don't be late."

"Okay," I say.

"I'll be there," agrees Lawrence.
And then it's time to prepare for supper.

CHAPTER 19

Kate

August, 1849

The next morning, Sarah comes to our wagon in tears. "Luke is sick. He couldn't get warm all night. What should I do?"

"I'll go back with you to see what can be done," says Mama. The two women hurry back to Sarah's wagon. Mama puts her arm around Sarah in a comforting way. She's good at that.

"Let's start a fire," says Grandma. "I need some tea after that news."

"Grandma, what are you thinking?" I ask.

"Let's wait for your Mama to return, and then we'll talk about what I'm thinking."

Mama comes back looking pale and worried. "There'll be no more traveling until we see about Luke. Grandma, I'm so glad you got the fire started. I could use some tea myself."

"Mama, can we help? What's Luke got?" I ask.

"You can help by caring for Kate, Daniel and Lily. I stopped by the Smith wagon, and they have room for all them to sleep. We're going to keep the children away from Luke until he's well."

"Mama, what is it?" I ask again, afraid of the answer.

"It seems like the cholera. He's in a coma and his fever is high.

"Good Lord, I had a feeling it was cholera," says Bertie. "Shall I go with the cooling compresses, Louisa?"

"Let's wait until the children come. Sarah will send them here soon as they wake."

We wait breakfast until the children arrive.

"We have a whole day to play. What would you like to do, Kate?" I ask her, trying to act like nothing is different.

"Can we go back to the Rock? Maybe we can find another feather bed for me."

"Sounds good to me. And we can carve our names on the Rock, too. David, do you have a good carving stone?"

"I do. Kate, Daniel and Lily have one, too. Remember when I gave you each a stone yesterday? They were strong stones that scratch granite. Bring them along and we'll each carve a name."

"I know where mine is," calls Kate and before we can stop her, she runs to her wagon.

By the time I reach the wagon, I hear Sarah scolding Kate in a loud voice.

"Why are you back here? Don't you know your Papa is very ill? No, you can't get the stone from the valuables box. Now, go back to Emelie and the others."

"But, Mama . . ."

"Did you hear me? Now go."

I think Luke's sickness is worrying her. I've never heard her raise a voice to her children. What a terrible strain to care for a sick husband and have three little ones, too.

When Kate comes from the wagon, I know what to do.

"Kate, you won't need a stone after all. David has so many, maybe hundreds and hundreds of them. The stone can stay right where you put it, just come along. We have to carve names today. Today is an important day."

She takes my hand and walks quietly beside me. We find the others all ready to go. Slowly we begin our trek up the side of the big Rock called Independence.

"I looked the place over yesterday," says David. We'll have to climb higher than we were to find a place where all our names can be together."

"David, you be the leader. Is that okay with you, Kate?"

"Yes," she whispers.

We walk along, slower than the others. It's almost like she's the sick one of our group.

"I have an idea. Would you like to find something special today for your Papa? He would like that." I'm hoping this works to help her forget Sarah's scolding. She's quiet for a moment. I take a deep breath.

"Oh yes, Emelie. Maybe what I find will make him better?"

"Of course it will. Now let's go catch up with the others."

"There are those men again," Kate pulls me towards the Latter Day Saints we saw yesterday. "Would they have something nice for Papa?"

"Today let's look for something your Papa hasn't seen yet. Remember you and he went strolling yesterday looking for musical instruments. He probably saw everything then. We want this to be a surprise for him. And, look up there, David is ready for us now."

We climb and climb until I feel I'm on top of the world.

"Looky here," David calls down to us. "Another David wrote his name in '42."

"Is my name on a rock already?" asks Kate.

"No, I haven't seen any 'Kate' here, but very soon there will be a 'Kate.' Your own name."

She sits beside me and watches. I try to master printing on this rough surface with a stone my brother says is the best for carving. "K—A—T—E says your name," I say as the letters slowly appear.

"Four letters is all I have?"

"Four important letters," I say. "They will be here forever. Everyone who rides by this place will see them and know you've been here."

"Will they know you were here, too?"

"Yes, because my name is going right next to yours."

"That's very good." She is so happy I get a hug for my labor.

"Watch this, Kate. I'm going to draw a heart."

But Kate is ready to move on and so I follow her to where David and Cora Jo are playing with Daniel and Lily.

"Would you please watch Kate for me? I want to go back to the Rock and carve something else there," I say.

"Sure, we're having fun," David answers.

As I climb back up to where we left our names, I take time to notice how deep blue the sky is above me and how gray-green the sagebrush below. In the distance, there are rounded tops of land but none as high as this Independence Rock. I like to think of its other name: The Register of the Desert.

The lack of trees makes everything visible and open as far as I can see. Quietness is everywhere. I feel like I am miles from the discarded items, the Latter Day Saints, and the sick Luke.

I find our carving place and take David's stone. I work hard forming the letters. When I'm finished, I feel a calmness at what I've done.

"Emelie, look what I've found!" Kate's voice brings me back as I see a bright golden coin in her small palm.

We take the coin to Stephen. He turns it over and over. "It has a raised cross on it. The Spaniards were Catholic like us. I'll bet it's real gold!"

"Kate, your Papa will be so proud of you when you show him," I say.

"Let's go, Emelie. We'll show him and he'll get better."

On the way back, Kate talks about her father and the games he played with her. Because she is all but five years old and the oldest of the three, she got special attention from her Papa. I can tell by listening how much she loves him.

It is quiet when we get there. I remember Sarah's harshness, so I remind Kate to be very quiet when she gets into the wagon. I go in first.

I see Sarah lying near Luke, weeping. "Kate found something for Luke," I whisper.

Kate crawls to her Mama and hugs her, but her big brown eyes are on her father. She is still holding the coin tightly in her hand.

"Papa," she says. "Look what I got you. Papa?"

"He's dead, Kate. Your coin isn't any good. Take it away, leave me alone!"

"Papa, don't die. I got this coin for you," Kate cries. "Papa, don't die. Papa! Papa!"

"Go away, child."

I watch this child and her mother. My strength leaves me. I can't move.

"Emelie, take her away." Sarah closes her eyes. Her arms hold Luke tightly as she puts her head on his chest to be even closer to her husband.

Kate begins to sob, the kind that makes her breath come in spasms. I pick her up and wonder if I have enough strength to make it outside.

I carry her to our wagon and nearly collapse with exhaustion. "Mama, come. Luke is dead."

It takes hours for the men to dig the grave deep in this hard-packed soil—deep to discourage scavenging wolves and pilfering Indians.

Sarah doesn't want to let Luke go. We allow her to mourn for a day, then Bertie gives her laudanum to relax her, and when she sleeps we remove the body from the wagon.

Luke was our musician. He gave Lawrence and me our first lesson just the other evening. He was a good Papa to his children. Mama always said life wasn't fair. I heard it enough to be used to it, but I'm not.

Strung out on the Trail are weather-beaten planks or stones marking the place of a death that broke someone's heart. If death should take me, I'll be left here, as well.

In my memory is the day we buried Tim. There was light dancing on the green grass beneath the trees. A bird's song trilled somewhere above. The clouds were white fluffs against the deep blue sky. I look about me. This landscape is different. No trees. No birds. No clouds. Bright light that makes one squint bathes the prairie. I feel the dry sand beneath my feet. The prairie dogs come to watch. They look like they're praying, too.

After Luke is in his resting place and the prayer is said, I close my eyes and hear Papa's deep voice say, "No one needs to keep watch this night. There is nothing that can harm us more than did our most recent trial." Our wagons move over and over the freshly dug soil to fool our eyes into thinking no one is there.

I notice that Papa doesn't fuss about time anymore. He never speaks about crossing the Sierras before the first snowfall. I think the energy is snuffed out of him like a blown-out candle.

One day on the way to Fort Bridger, the last stop before Deseret, the boys find a cool spring. I take it upon myself to invite Sarah to bathe. She has isolated herself from us since Luke's death. Maybe water will help.

I lift the wagon cover and look around. Where once a large mattress covered the floor, with playthings scattered on top for the children, there are now piles of clothing—rags—I can't even tell which, such a huge heap they make. Sarah, in her grief, keeps to her same soiled clothing day after day.

I gently shake her and call her name. She wakes and sits up, eyes still closed, hair plastered to one cheek.

"Sarah, the boys found a spring. Your children are splashing around. Won't you come?"

"Get out of here," she moans, lies back down, and rolls away from me.

"Sarah, your children miss you." Sarah remains facing the wagon cover.

"Sarah," I say as I rub her back. "Sarah, do you hear me? Do you?" My words are not heeded. Sarah remains in her own world, far away from mine.

I jump from the wagon and run to the spring. I feel the cool dampness as I approach. If our sadness could vanish as easily as we go from the desert heat into the coolness of

WEST TO THE ELEPHANT

the glade, I think it would be better for us than any gold we may find. I wonder what has happened to the gold coin that Kate found for her Papa. It surely kept its luck inside itself.

CHAPTER 20

Deseret

August, 1849

O ur entry into Deseret is spectacular. The Great Salt Lake sparkles green in the distance, looking huge like an ocean. Papa tells us it's saltier. Over it, a weather pattern performs for us. Two black thunderheads, one over the south section of the lake, the other over the snow-capped Wasatch Range compete for my attention. The lightning flashes first from one then from the other. And over in the West the sun is bringing out a rainbow. The lake glitters with both the sun and the lightning. I can't stop looking at it.

Cora Jo breaks out into a rainbow song, "Violet, indigo, blue and green, yellow, orange and red." I can see every color she sings in the bright, bright color there in the sky. Deseret will be a good place for Sarah and for us. The restless sky is speaking for the land below it. I feel its power. I close my eyes, breathe deeply, and know God is with us.

Now comes the hard part—the walk down a mountainside into the city of Deseret below. Rocky slopes, gullies carved into the soil, dead branches left by the wind all interfere with our descent. I hear Papa shouting at his sons who are pulling back on the oxen towing Sarah's wagon.

"Pull back, boys, pull back! Remember, the Saints said this mountainside is steeper than we think."

I have Josie to walk down the steep decline. Mama has Brown. Papa has our wagon.

"Emelie, is Josie making it okay?"

"Yes, Mama, I'm pulling her back and she's listening to me really well," I shout. That's the only way one gets heard in this land of big spaces.

"Good. If you need help, call me. Watch those rocks, don't want you to turn your ankle."

Our descent takes the whole day. Tired as we are, the first stop we make is with Sarah in mind. The boys have ridden ahead and found the meetinghouse where emigrants are welcomed and given a host family for their stay in Deseret.

"They're planning a hospital to quarantine those who are ill," my brothers come out to tell us. "It's not ready yet, but there's a physician who'll see Sarah. Do you think we might help Sarah walk in there?"

"We can try," says Bertie, but she doesn't sound optimistic.

I leave the group when Mama and Grandma Bertie go into the wagon to help remove Sarah. I see that the wideness of the street allows wagons to make a turnaround with ease. Such an idea, I think. Back home we need streets like these.

The sound of running water here in high desert country takes me by surprise. I follow the sound to see small canals of running water behind the houses. Each house seems to have its own supply. Could that be why the gardens are green and flowery, and why the barns are filling up with sweet-smelling hay?

"No. No. No." I hear Sarah's voice shouting as clear as day. I'm embarrassed by this outburst. To be noisy in this quiet place makes us look obviously different. Will there always be something? I hurry back to see what's going to happen.

When Mama sees me walking quickly towards her, she says, "You heard her outburst? Papa is going to get the doctor to go to her wagon."

I take my place between Mama and Grandma. We wait, arms entwined, for the doctor's assessment of this sad, sad person. Cora Jo and David take her children for a walk around the meetinghouse. It's better for them to be on a stroll than to stand around waiting for a glimpse of their distraught Mama.

Papa comes over to us, squatting down on the hard dirt walkway. "I've been thinking, this stop may be a good thing for Sarah. We're not in so much of a rush that we can't linger long enough to urge her back into health. This is a very well organized city. There's bound to be help for her here, even more so than in California."

"Good, Eugene. I was hoping we could stay for Sarah's sake. It will do us all good to see her well again."

"We just heard that the animals and wagons will have to be corralled away from the townspeople during our stay. The corral is at the foot of Main Street. Emelie and Stephen can drive Sarah's wagon there, get the oxen unyoked to roam freely, then walk back to the guest house," Papa tells us.

"Bertie, would you mind spending tonight with Sarah in the wagon if she refuses the hospitality in the guest house that's been offered?" asks Mama. "There's no one else Sarah seems to trust like you."

"What about me? She trusts me, Mama. I've been in her wagon many times playing with her children. Let me stay with her and give dear Grandma Bertie a break."

A surprise comes over us all as a small voice asks, "Can I see my Mama now?" It's Kate and she looks as though she's been crying.

"Of course, Kate," I say. I take her by the hand, tell her to be very quiet, and lift her into Sarah's wagon. I jump up to follow her and see Sarah still on the mattress that now has even more things on it than before.

Kate creeps towards her and reaches over to touch her arm. The next thing I see is Kate being slapped so hard she lands near me. I comfort her as best as I can while her Mama sits staring out the back of the wagon towards the mountains. I whisper her name, but there's no response. I carry Kate to our guest house, where everyone is discussing what may be best to help Sarah out of her sadness.

"I'm afraid that any change will set her back some. It's Bertie she's used to."

"And besides," says Bertie, smiling once again, "I'm fit as a fiddle for this nursing work. Sarah and I have an understanding now. She allows me to rub her arms and legs each morning. She's even still when I sponge her off, although I've not been able to get to her hair. Don't worry a bit. I'll let you know when I'm ready for some time off. Just plan on me spending the night in Sarah's wagon. Heaven knows, this old body is used to sleeping quarters in wagons."

The physician, a tall thin man with a somber face, comes out of the wagon. I wonder how anyone who looks so grim could ever be the bearer of good news. I brace myself for the worst.

"This woman has a serious case of hysteria. She's not contagious, but I'd watch her closely. She's capable of doing something hurtful to herself or others."

God in heaven," Mama exclaims. "Isn't there anything you can give her?"

"No. Nothing. Time is the best healer."

"It looks like we're all going to help care for Sarah. Bertie, it's not right for you to carry the whole burden," Mama says, looking squarely into her face. "We'll just plan to continue on our journey and have Sarah repair with time. There doesn't seem to be anything else to do."

We all look at Mama, not saying a word. The disappointment is heavy around us. Yet, no one protests Mama's desire to continue. "Emelie, can I count on you to get to Sarah's wagon early so Bertie can come with me to the marketplace? We have the ninety-mile desert to get ready for next. After we've gotten our supplies, we'll come up with a plan to care for Sarah as we continue our journey."

Stephen and I walk Grandma back to Sarah's wagon. We straighten up a bit so Grandma Bertie has a place free from all the clothes that are strewn about. We say nothing to Sarah as she stares out the back of the wagon.

"Grandma Bertie, is there anything we can get you from our wagon or the guest house before you and Sarah sleep for the night?"

"No, child. Just convince your Mama to let you go instead of me tomorrow to the market. My place is with Sarah."

"You know Mama. I'll be here in the morning, Bertie."

I lean over Sarah, who's facing away from us, and kiss her on the cheek. I notice her eyes are open and her fists are balled up under her chin. She hardly looks like she's ready to sleep. "Goodnight, Sarah. Sleep well tonight," I whisper.

The guest house is a pleasure after our time on the Trail. The sheets on the bed Cora Jo and I share have been ironed and smell fresh, like mountain air. Grandma would enjoy this comfort. Sarah would, too, if she were well. She has changed so much from the time she helped birth little Adam. She and Luke were close. Grandma and her Bertie were close. Susan and Tim were, too. What causes this illness with some and not others?

As I lie on my side of this comfortable bed, I am fidgety. I can see Sarah's sleeping children all crowded into the bed next to ours. The steady breaths of all do not lull me into my own sleep. Outside choruses of frogs shout accusations and grasses rustle like whispers. The night sounds take hold and clarify a thought of mine. I think of all the times Sarah surprised me. During river crossings she stayed in her wagon; she didn't eat with us at Mormon Crossing; her shortness with Kate after she found the gold coin; her temper tonight when she slapped Kate. It's not because she's a widow. No, it started before that, while Luke was still alive. There's something about Sarah and her anger. I want to know more. If I only knew where to begin.

I'm filled with such disquiet I have trouble lying still.

I can't wait for morning. I'm going to the corral now. If Sarah is sleeping, I'll lie next to Grandma and wait for morning.

The evening air is cool and refreshing on my sweaty body. In the bright moonlight I notice the houses are mostly adobe, like the forts we've stopped at. And, like the forts, there are wooden roofs. But here and there some are covered with earth, looking quaint as a fairy tale. I'm glad the animals are quiet as I approach.

A fence post is broken that I'm sure will be mended before the day is over. I enter through that opening and walk past many wagons, all unhitched from their oxen. I remember the last time I walked past so many. It was in hot and dusty St. Joseph and I was looking for Cora Jo. Deseret is pleasantly cool and green. The other thing I like is that it's as close to California as we've ever been.

I spot Sarah's wagon with its distinctive kettle hanging out the rear. If the moonlight were not so bright, I might have had trouble.

"Grandma! Sarah!" My loud whisper gets no answer. I hoist myself up to the driver's bench and move the cover aside. I can make out Grandma lying down, but Sarah is not there! I think my heart will jump out of my chest any second. I swallow and think fast. Sarah must be somewhere in the corral.

I stand for a few moments surveying the small community of animals and wagons. There is a slight movement over yonder. In my eagerness, I walk towards it. The figure becomes clearer. It is Sarah, hair flowing in the breeze, soiled clothing covering her thin body.

"Sarah! Sarah! Wait. It's me, Emelie." I reach out to stop her.

"No. I want to die." She looks at the ground, but she stops.

"You're not going to die. Come now, before we waken the whole of Deseret from this corral."

I begin to pull her back. To my surprise, it is no trouble pulling this deranged, frail person. I'm able to put my arm around her and hold her as we walk back. She slips down and leans on the wagon wheel and sobs, her face in her hands.

"Sarah, what's the matter? Tell me. I can help." I whisper.

She shakes her head over and over. I know I must ask her. And yet, I don't want to set her back in her sickness. I wish Bertie were here right now. Or even Cora Jo. Most of all I don't want her to yell out like a crazy woman.

"Sarah, I want to ask you about Grandma's box."

"Arggggh," she croaks.

"Sarah, the box. Do you know where it is?" I'm whispering as softly as I can.

"I wanted to help Luke, my husband. I loved him so much. He worked on buildings, hands cramping up with the cold, skin splitting with chap, back aching with the lifting. So hard . . . worked all his life." She mumbles, sobbing. I take my apron to wipe her teary face and hold her.

"Land. Gold. He had never known an easy life. I wanted to give it to him and now I've been punished for my wrongdoing. God took away the only thing that ever mattered to me."

"Sarah, don't talk like that. God doesn't punish. He made you a mother and gave you three children to love. If you allow, you can return the box yourself to Grandma Bertie. She will understand and forgive you. You'll see."

"Bertie?" Sarah screams. "She has lived the life of privilege. She had her husband until they grew old together. God has always been on her side. Riches, travels, a lifelong companion. What more could she want?"

I believe we are waking up the animals with her tirade. I speak softly to calm her.

"She wanted children. She called them a blessing."

I push Sarah's hair back from her damp forehead. I wipe her face again. Her paleness is startling in the moonlight, and underneath her closed eyes, dark half circles add a somber look.

I hug her to let her know that I understand. She doesn't respond. I caress her hands as we sit there together on the soft dried grasses that cover the ground of the corral. What a terrible thing she has endured all these weeks. Sarah was living a lie, a deception that is making her mad. I make the sign of the cross for her forgiveness and for me, in thanksgiving. I'm free of my heavy burden. Grandma Bertie will have her California dream back. Sarah took the box. We'll find it in her wagon!

Sarah begins to shiver.

"You're cold," I say. "I'll be right back."

Slowly, I disengage myself and go to the wagon. I move the cover and scan the inside of the wagon for a blanket. Grandma is still sleeping. This time the moon's light fills the wagon. I see something I cannot comprehend. Moving closer, the horror I see weakens me. Blood is seeping from the side of Grandma's head. And the box! The cursed box is lying on its side, contents spilling out.

I scream. I can't stop. My voice belongs to someone else. Soon the wagon is filled with torchlight. Strangers are peering into the wagon. A large man comes in and kneels down to look at Grandma. "She's breathing," he says. Then he glares at me. "Say, miss. Can you tell me what happened?"

I can't talk; I'm too frightened. Then my voice comes. "Sa—rah!" I yell and get up to look for her outside the wagon.

"Jest a minute, now. Where do you think you're going?" The man is now holding me back.

"Sarah! She knows," I say as clearly as I can, but it doesn't sound right to me. "I must go to her."

"Where is this Sarah? She's not outside the wagon," he says, still holding me fast.

"She's not? She's not? Let me go, I must find her!"

But the group surrounds me. They aren't letting me through. They think I did this to Grandma. Oh, dear God, where is Sarah? Where are Mama and Papa?

I come to my senses. I'm not guilty, and I will not be browbeaten into such a feeling. "Dear God," I pray silently, "please help me." I go to where Grandma is lying and kneel down next to her. "Grandma, I'm here. It's me, Emelie. You're going to be fine. I'll see to it. We're going to get a doctor. Grandma, your box is here. Did you hear me? Your box is here."

Now I look the group over. Actually, there are only five or six of them. I say, strongly now, "Do any of you have any water? I want to wipe Grandma's head."

I hear one woman say, "I'll fetch some." And she leaves.

"I'll tell you what happened," I say, surprising myself with my calmness, and I notice they all pay attention.

CHAPTER 21

Grandma Bertie

Early September, 1849

The doctor has sewn the skin on Bertie's scalp together and the bleeding has stopped. She is snug on the fragrant white sheets in the bed I left last evening. Dark lids hide her bright eyes. That's okay. They need a rest from the world that injured her. Her once tight ringlets seem relaxed, like they are too weak to spring back. But I know they will. She just needs time.

"The heavy blow caused insensibility. Don't know how long she'll be in the coma . . . ." The doctor was talking, but I interrupted. I asked permission to be in the bedroom with my Grandma. And here I sit. I'll wait until she wakes from the blow to her head. I want her to see me first.

I take her hands in mine. They are cool. They need to be warm and full of life. I rub them gently and put my cheek on them for good measure. How different these calloused hands are from the hands of the fine lady I met in Philadelphia. The bits of soil and sand under nails and in her hair and clothing make her look like all of us who are making the Westward journey.

"Emelie, are you all right?" Mama comes into the room, quietly as only she can. "I want you to rest. I'll sit with Bertie. Why don't you lie on the other bed?"

She slips her arm around me and we both look at Grandma Bertie for a few moments. Then I hug my Mama, grateful that she is still here. I go to the other bed, hoping that sleep will take some of the terrible thoughts from my mind. Luke's death, Grandma Bertie's injury, Sarah, the box. I just want to sleep it all away.

When I awake, it is dark again. It was dark when I left my bed last evening—the worst evening of my life, for sure. I look towards Grandma's bed. It's empty, the sheets and pillows have been removed. Puzzled, I run into the hallway looking for Mama.

Voices are coming from the first floor. I skip down the steps and see our group sitting around the parlor: the Smiths, the Solvaines, the Rhysses. Stephen and David are sitting on the floor with Cora Jo. Mama has Sarah's children about her. They all turn to look at me, and at that moment Maria takes Sarah's children from Mama. A tiredness washes over me and my breath comes in short spurts. I barely pant out my question, "Where's Grandma?"

Mama puts her arms around me. "Darling, the blow to her head was too hard and too deep."

"Mama, I didn't say goodbye to her," I hear myself screaming, as I pull away from her grasp. "I want Bertie. She can't be dead. Not my Bertie. I want to say goodbye to her. I want to say goodbye to her."

I push Mama away. My arms wave like a mad woman's, ready for anyone else who dares come near me. "Where is she?" My voice screams like it belongs to another. The howling strains my throat and I cough, down deep into my belly. I feel arms restrain me. Strong. Papa's. I give in.

I vaguely remember a funeral. Stephen and Lawrence stand beside me, very close, their arms around me as if to hold me up. The music is soothing. I weep because I have no control over my tears; they just come despite my numbness. The burial is held in a cemetery for Gentiles. Grandma would have said something about that. As the soil covers her casket, I know she will always be here. How strange that her assailant will always be here, too. Sarah's body was found by Latter Day Saints on their way to farm the upper meadows.

We leave Deseret the next day. From the wagon I see the tidiness of the wide streets. The gardens are still flowering and full of color despite late August. I look closely at every detail, so my mind will remember this, too, and not only the misery of what happened here. I look up and see the Wasatch Range rising above the city. These are the mountains that beckoned Sarah. She stared at them over and over again, but never made it to their protective cover.

Bertie and I planned to walk to the Great Salt Lake before we continued on our journey. We wanted to feel its briny waters on our feet, see the wildlife come to its shores and marvel at its size. One day I will come back. I will follow the plan dearest Bertie and I made and give thanks to the Lord for having given her to me even for so short a time.

September 1849

Dearest Aden,
So much of my life has changed since I wrote you last. It was in Deseret that we found and lost the thief. It was Sarah, who stole the box and murdered our dearest Grandma. Murdered our Grandma Bertie. I know I wrote that twice. Maybe if I see the words, their darkness will yield some light of understanding to my simple mind. Each waking moment, my mind's eye is filled with Grandma's sweet face. Even today, I hear her lively voice and the quips she filled us with on this long journey.
I'm too tired to write more.
Emelie

CHAPTER 22

Frank and Vince

September, 1849

Papa was told that the ninety-mile trip across the Great Salt Desert had no water source at all. If my tears were drinking water, we would have had enough. I listened to the plans, but my sorrow prevented me from taking part. We would travel day and night with only 15-minute stops to rest. The desert must be traversed quickly. Each of the families had their own food supply, which was prepared with the help of the Mormon women. Nothing had to be cooked.

"We're testing your mettle," says Papa. I notice no one laughs at this like they once did.

We had heard it before. We had been tested and came away stronger for it, or were we just more experienced?

As I look up at the sky, I see clouds with patches of deep blue above us. It had rained during the night, and the moisture was keeping the dust down. Mama had the scarves ready for our noses and mouths for when it got unbearable.

In my mind Mama's words were speaking to me about the next part of the journey, "As long as we're together, everything will be fine." We aren't fine. We're missing someone dear to us. I don't ask, but believe that Mama would change what she said so long ago.

"Emelie," I hear Mama's soft voice. "We'll be moving out shortly. All the families will be caring for the Smith children. We'll take turns keeping them. Our turn will come when we're on the other side of this desert."

I nod. Mama was getting me ready. She's giving me 90 miles to mourn, 90 miles to put Bertie in the past, 90 miles to remember without weeping. I will try.

The drinking water is monitored. We know the water barrels we are carrying have to last four days. The oxen need water more than we. They pull our life belongings for us. They are the reason we could make this trip at all. By the second evening, Mama notices we have only two barrels left. We drink sparingly always waiting for evening and the refreshing coolness it brings.

After two days and two nights of constant travel, it begins to show. Our catnaps don't renew us. There are no trees to add shadows to the landscape, not a bird to cheer neither us nor animals to excite us. The days are all blinding white that stretches into the horizon from any direction. If Natives are here, they stay in their oasis, a place we don't know and never find.

Cora Jo wakes from a nap, cranky. Nothing suits her. She moves over to Mama and puts her thumb in her mouth. She's eleven. What has this journey done to us?

Mama is always ready to "lap" any one of us. The big ones she pulls down and hugs us around the waist, then lets us go. Cora Jo is the one who goes to Mama most frequently. Warm lap, cuddly Mom whispering soft love words to her youngest daughter—her "BG."

What the boys and I called her when she was annoying back home was very different: P-I-G, to which she would let out a howl as loud as anything a human can produce. Then amidst her tears, we would get scolded for teasing her. Of course, after the scolding was finished and Mama left, giggles were always in order. Why didn't we understand how Cora Jo hurt?

Funny how these thoughts creep into my mind in this lonesome place.

We watch as Cora Jo moves to be comforted by Mama. If anything we are all thinking how we wished we could be there, too, on Mama's lap, feeling her softness, smelling her fragrance—which is more soil, dust, and sweat now—but still gives the feeling of comfort.

By midday the sand is dry and dust is blowing onto the drivers and into the wagon itself. As it blows, it erases any signs that human or animal life had traveled West before us. At our short stop, a fellow traveler gave us fresh plums and apricots. I could hear Grandma say, "Why this is a little bit of heaven to enjoy."

When I see my brothers splashing the oxen's nostrils and eyelids with water, and see my sister doing the same with our horses and mules, I help. Cora Jo smiles a "thanks" to me.

Mirages keep appearing out there on the horizon. Shimmering wavy light looking like steam from a kettle of boiling water causes us to tap each other and point to the sight our eyes and minds had created. Sometimes I see bushes waving in the distance and feel they are real, until we get close. Sometimes they turn out to be shadows of the sand hills before us, sometimes a depression blown out by the wind. Only here do shadows change what is real. One view from a distance, another from close by.

Yes, I thought, this is a valley of death, and I marvel at how Papa was navigating this open land with not one wagon track to follow. My dear Grandma would be pleased.

Papa decides to travel the Hastings Cutoff to the Ruby Mountains. It was good for me to see the ground rise above us once again. The spotty snow on the peaks promised cool water for us down below. The change in temperature revives me and this time when Lawrence comes to our wagon to see how I am, I'm ready to walk a bit with him.

"No rivers, no water. This is a horrible place," says Cora Jo. "I'm tired of stale bread with vinegar. Wish we'd find more berries."

"Think we'll ever find a river with good-eating fish?" I ask Lawrence.

"Sure we will, but don't ask me when. It's got to be somewhere."

"I see," I say. "Maybe the fish will be right in there with the gold waiting for us in California." I said the words, but they were Bertie's. I've heard her optimism during times like these. I will always remember this about her.

I see smiles appearing on the faces of our disappointed traveling companions, and I knew I had said a good thing.

"I'm sorry about Bertie," he says.

"Thank you."

"I'm sorry about Sarah, too." His voice is soft and comforting.

"It's so hard for me to comprehend all that has happened. I wish I could sleep it all away and never wake up."

"Well, you sure did a good job of sleeping. You've been sleeping for nigh on a week."

"I bet I haven't missed much—heat, dust, desert. Just the same, every day. It's dear, dear Bertie I miss."

"I know. I'm here to help you push that back of your head. We have a lot of traveling yet to do. We got be helpful to each other."

I'm quiet.

And as if a miracle happened, a fresh-water spring bubbles at the first rise from the desert sands.

"Looky over there, Emelie. Is that wet on the rocks?"

"Let's go see!" Suddenly I felt free after the stifling desert crossing. Heat and tears seemed to cool off and disappear from me at that moment.

"Lawrence, I think we should climb to find the water source."

We climb by holding on to saplings and making footholds in the soft mountain soil. The gurgling of the water beckons us higher. When I see the fresh stream rushing down the mountain side, I run to it, cupping my hands and drinking deeply. My thirst quenched, I rub the blessed wetness all over my arms, face and neck. It is dripping down into my bodice before I stop.

"Now this is my Emelie!" I hear him say. "Do you know you are laughing?"

"Oh, Lawrence! Is there anything as refreshing as cool, clear water?"

"A good meal," he smiles.

"You're not wet enough, your brain is dried out and not thinking properly!"

Then I splash him as I might have splashed my brothers in another time and place. Giggling and laughing as he came toward me, my instinct was to run. But before I even raised myself from the rock, he encircles me with his arms and swings me around. Now I'm laughing harder.

"That will teach you not to splash!" he says.

He sets me down gently and smoothes my hair back from my face. I look at him, hair dripping water, wetness making streaks on his dusty face, and I knew, just by looking, he was going to kiss me!

It was a long, sweet kiss. I felt the warmth of him after the coolness of the water. The excitement of the climb and the water play had relaxed me into pleasure. We stayed close for a long while, not speaking. I smelled his manly aroma. It was different from Aden's, perhaps a bit hardier, more acrid and earthy, but pleasant. The sound of the water sliding, tumbling, plunging down over the rocks and stones brought me back to reality.

"That's what I call refreshing!" he says while squeezing me tightly. "Let's tell the others what we've found."

I nod. That's about all I can manage.

The children run to get towels and catch the water running down the rocky mountain side. When they are completely wet from head to toe, they twist water from the towels and fling them at each other. Only after everyone enjoys this respite, does our caravan move on.

Papa knows that we are approaching the Wells of the Humboldt, the pleasant moisture after the desert. He tells us that a long respite will be waiting for us soon as we see the river.

It is a slow and difficult ascent through the foothills of the ridges before the Ruby Mountains. The wagons move so close to the edge of the precipice, I want to call out to Papa. I don't and keep this worry to myself. When I see our oxen displace rocks and stones in their path, I feel they are getting clumsy and tired like all of us. Not too long after that, Papa wants to free the oxen from the burden of carrying us and the wagons, too. So we walk, climbing up and up and trying not to turn our ankles on the stones hidden beneath our feet.

Lawrence walks with me many times, and each time I suggest we "adopt" one of the children traveling with us. I take one by the hand, and he carries one high up on his shoulders. The parents seem pleased and the children are absolutely delighted with the made-up games and fun antics we provide for them.

The cool evenings awaken us enough to forget our tiredness, and with no level ground to make camp, we continue on. Men and boys carry torches made of dried sagebrush. The fragrance is fresh and energizing. This night we walk until daybreak and feel the joy that comes with being over the pass and at the refreshing water of the South Fork of the Humboldt River.

We untie the oxen and watch them graze lazily among the grasses of the river bank. We pull the horses to the wheat of the river meadow. The mules? They wander wherever they wish, but always stay clear of damp ground. Just like Papa says, "Mules don't like wet feet!"

"Come, help make a fire, everyone. We must boil the water so it doesn't sicken us."

"Mama, can't we rest first?" I plead. "I believe we'll fall asleep tending the fire."

"Emelie, water first, sleep last."

So we gather twigs, branches, even small tree limbs and make a bonfire. Everyone brings kettles of water that we set on the fire. Sleep at last. When we wake, the water will be purified enough to drink.

I'm dreaming, but no, I hear some feet shuffling nearby. There, around our makeshift camp, a tribe of Natives is touching our possessions and seem curious about everything we had put on the ground. Up on my elbows I see Mama and Papa and others of the caravan ready to trade with these Natives. I'm wondering what they have that's worth trading for.

"I would like what you have," Mama says, pointing to the buckets of fish they are carrying.

"Mama," I say, "would David's stones attract them enough to trade?"

"Good idea, Emelie. David, would you go get them?"

"Mama, what do they have that you want?" I ask.

"Buckets of minnows. Fresh. Just waiting to be cooked and eaten."

David very carefully dumps his treasures on the ground. He fingers them with loving touches. Some sparkle in the bright sunlight. Soon a group of Natives gathers around to watch. David holds up one stone and with a smile holds it out to the group. Someone comes forward, takes it, laughs and moves away. Soon, all the Natives have one of David's stones, either one of a beautiful color or a shiny one that pleases them. They leave us the bucket of minnows and leave quietly.

"That's not a fair trade," I say.

"It must be, Emelie. Have you noticed how the Pawnee and Sioux carved stone and bone for jewelry? Their handiwork is to be admired."

"Dave, you came to the rescue again. Thanks, son!" says Papa, as he tousles David's already messy hair. "I do believe those were the Digger Indians, ones who dig roots and tubers for their food. Obviously they fish, too."

"Mama, I'll get the fry pans." My stomach is thinking that those little shiny things may taste good. The boys run to find dry sagebrush for our fire as I walk to our mules for the pans.

Before long the boys return to our campsite with more than just sagebrush—two men dirty as all outdoors but smiling like they just saw heaven.

"Good day, all you nice folks. This is a miracle for certain that we found you out in these wide open spaces. I'm Vince, and this here is Frank. And we've been walking a long, long time." Frank points to his worn shoes as Vince continues. "Now we didn't mean to be walkin' or we would have had on our hiking clothes . . ."

"Yeah, our expensive hiking clothes that are a-sittin' in a wagon stuck in the mud somewheres East of here . . . ."

"You look like you've come a long way . . . come sit with us," says Mama, inviting them with her smile. "We'll have a good supper in a while, and you are welcome to join us."

"Don't be timid now, have some fresh water and rest a bit. We want to hear your story over supper," Papa adds.

These jolly, very dirty men, each find a tree trunk, place their rucksacks as pillows and within a moment are snoring away. I wonder at the tales they will have when they wake.

It's so strange to find folks out here in the wilds of the West, that we scurry around to help with the meal and look forward to the conversation we'll have when they awake. There isn't a sound as we hear their story.

"Have any of you folks heard of the Pioneer Line?" No one has, so Vince explains. It's a company of wagons that travel west from Independence."

"It's not cheap, but they promise comfortable travel all the way to the gold country. So we bought ourselves a couple of tickets," says Frank.

"How large is the company?" asks Papa.

"Twenty passenger carriages and twenty-two for luggage and supplies. We made quite a long train," Vince said.

"And how long was it supposed to take from Independence?" Papa asks.

"The time is what really sold us. They promised to get us to the gold country two months sooner than the usual five months of travel. We were ready! But what a surprise we were in for. The new elliptical springs that cushioned our carriages got stuck in the boggy banks of the Platte." Frank says.

"So there we were, in a comfortable carriage that wouldn't budge an inch!" adds Vince.

"I know how bad that can be," says Papa. "We've always been careful to keep to the current and move quickly."

"Have you kept to walking the Trail since the Platte River stalled the wagons?" asks Mama.

"I'm afraid so. Frank and I took a wagon outfitted with mules. With two other friends, we proceeded Westward. By the time we got to the Wells of the Humboldt, the two were ill, and we decided to wait out their sickness there. It was a pleasant spot mainly because of the water and plentiful grasses," Vince says.

I see how this remembering fills his eyes with tears.

Frank breaks the silence, "Our acquaintances passed away within days of each other. We gave our mules to help pull another wagon with some elderly folks. We each took our rucksacks, stuffed them with a knife, a pistol, two blankets and our canteens. We've been traveling on foot ever since." Now tears are streaming down Frank's cheeks, clearing the dust in two straight lines from his eyes to his chin. I feel I'm intruding so I look away.

From then on, Frank and Vince are part of our caravan. We share everything with them despite the meagerness of our own provisions. They work hard to "earn their keep" and provide enjoyment by the many stories they have to tell.

Our group is now comprised of 17 adults and five children. Mama said we are blessed to have traveled together without discord and cantankerousness which could have made the wagon train an uncomfortable place to be.

The next morning we are packed and ready to leave at sunrise. We are anticipating a difficult trek. The Ruby Mountains are higher than the Rockies were at the South Pass. As I look at the jagged edges of yellow rock, they seem to say we are trespassers. Bertie would have something to say to them, I'm certain.

I feel the anxiety of our group as we anticipate a climb over the Ruby Mountains in the distance. Funny name—will we find red rubies?

It's difficult to relax and keep our attention on survival. As we walk in the coolness of the mornings and evenings, our appetites are continually awakened.

"We're gonna have some good eating soon," Lawrence says to me one day as we near the Humboldt River.

"I sure hope so. Are you thinking of fish?"

"Sure am," he says.

My stomach juices begin their readiness, as I quicken my pace to catch up to the oxen who are leading the train.

By the time Lawrence and I arrive at the head of the train, the oxen stop. Facing them is a stream of water moving as slow as molasses. The boys run to follow it, sometimes losing sight of the water in the tall grasses on the banks.

"What's this? Are there fish to catch? Is this where the minnows are," Mama asks. I can hear the impatience in her voice needing to know where the next meal is coming from.

"Louisa, you are looking at the Humboldt River," says Papa. "You'll get your minnows here. More good eating is on the way, folks!"

It's Frank who explains to Mama's satisfaction. "Your minnows, Ma'am, were from near where we are standin'. This is called the wells of the Humboldt. Here is where we best fill up if we want eatin' fish. Near the end, or the sink, the water will be almost stagnant before it disappears into a muddy hole in the ground. No fish swimmin' around there."

Mama looks relieved to know that there will be more fresh fish on the way West. I share her joy and know there is a smile on my face as I continue our trek.

We travel along the river bank. Lawrence notices that the Humboldt doesn't behave as the other rivers do.

"It's going East and West. The others flow north to South. Pap says it's the longest river we'll follow to California," Lawrence says as his eyes scan the river's ribbon of water.

"Frank, you know these parts better than we do. Does the Humboldt flow all the way to the ocean?" I ask, turning to our new friend who has just joined us.

"'Fraid not, no such luck. The river stops at a sink, which doesn't have the most pleasant smell around, we've heard. But by then we'll be right upon the Ruby Mountains, picking up all those rubies!"

I laugh and give our Frank a squeeze. He is so jolly and fun to be with during these long, long days. And the days are long. Being at the end is much worse than at the beginning. We are so anticipating the end of our travels we want to be there immediately.

"Listen, everyone, we've lost the river," Stephen calls out one day. "It seems to have disappeared into the ground. Papa is exploring the area now, to see if it's a good place to camp."

Oh! What rejoicing when we see the lush green grasses beckoning us to make camp. Other wagons are resting here, and the atmosphere is a happy one. I see Stephen and David chewing on young blades of grass as they cool off in the wetness of the ground.

Soon Lawrence is beside me. We're pleased with the young and tender grass, but the smell from the sink nearly makes us swoon. We don't even try to suck moisture from the green grass because of the scent of rotting grasses all around us. How curious that the grasses seem to disappear into the sink of the river. Nothing bothers the animals as they munch the green leaves. This hiatus is what they need, but it won't be long enough for their bloody hooves to heal. Papa wants us to be on the trail again in two days.

"Hey, there, Frank, I'm looking for those rubies you told us about. Think they may have fallen in the sink?"

"Why Miss Emelie, you think I was fooling you? Come on over to that slope and you will find rubies galore."

"Okay, I trust you. Come on everyone. Frank promises us rubies just over the slope. Let's go before they get taken away by greedy folks."

I hold my skirt to run up the incline, Lawrence is close behind me and soon others are following. With Frank in the lead, we go up and up, breathless until he stops.

"Here they are, young lass. Pick 'em until your fingers are stained red and your tummy is full."

"Oh, berries! Lots of berries. How did you know they were here?" I ask.

"When you read those travelin' books and know the hills and mountains, you can just figure on the berries being where they like to grow, whether in Pennsylvania or this here Western Territory," he says, laughing with all of us.

CHAPTER 23

Boiling Springs

Late September, 1849

It has become more pleasant to walk than ride despite the fact that I've laced my shoes on bottom to top. At least there is leather treading the ground. Bertie was so uncomplaining about all the inconveniences and hardships. I feel so badly when I take my complaining to our travelers. Today is one of those feet-hurt-complaining days.

"Lawrence, my feet hurt, but when I see our beasts of burden . . . ."

Lawrence interrupts, pointing skyward, "Looky there, Emelie. Vultures feeding."

I look up and see the huge black birds diving and rising above some prey. "Do you know what they are eating?"

"Dead animals. You know, when work becomes too hard and food becomes too sparse, they die."

"And folks leave them here to die? How sorry I am for them."

"Bet those Digger Indians are nearby and cut out their organs for themselves to feast on."

"Think so?"

"That's what they eat when they're not catchin' minnows. And maybe they only need an animal every once in a while. An animal is pretty big eating."

Mama suggests we stop in an area called Boiling Springs to soak our feet.

"The water won't be the swimming kind, but the warmth and the minerals will relieve our blisters and calluses. Heaven only knows when we'll be replacing our shoes."

The springs were indeed "boiling." They were much too hot for us to wade along its bank. But the next best thing was to dip some hot water and pour it slowly over our feet. It takes a while before the hot springs does its work. By the time we finish, our feet are positively tingling.

I watch Stephen put on his shoes. They are worse than mine. With two large holes in each sole, I know they will not last him the rest of the trip. I wonder how he had walked this far feeling every pebble and the hot sand. I think that if Mama and Papa had known of the miles of walking to be endured on this journey, they would have made us take three pairs of shoes each instead of two.

I walk over to my brother. "Stephen, wouldn't a squirrel skin work inside your shoes?" I say.

"I'm okay. Don't go saying anything."

There has to be something I can do. When he kicks off a shoe and holds up one foot, I see how the soles of his feet had toughened. Large yellow areas of hard skin are evident from the underside of his toes to his foot arch, and then again on to his heel.

I thought of the icy slopes that were still ahead. I could imagine a jagged rock penetrate his calloused skin. When I confided in Lawrence, he agreed to help in any way he could.

The ridge reluctantly yields its treasures. Many items that had been discarded along the way are now partially covered with sand and brush. We both brush away the top layers to see what is underneath. Papa said that as other emigrants found their animals becoming weaker, they lightened their load, just as we had done at the meadows. This is part of their treasure, left in the wilds.

"This is fun again," calls David. "It looks like what some folks left way back at Independence Rock, except there are more clothes here."

Lawrence and I both heard the word "clothes" and with a knowing glance at each other, decided to separate to scour the landscape looking for shoes.

I kicked at some of the items and found clothes that were hardly worn. Wouldn't it be nice to have another apron and discard the one I had worn since Deseret? I saw clothes that would fit Cora Jo, and wondered whether taking someone's clothes would be counted as a sin. I would be benefiting from someone's loss. This was one Church law that seemed not to matter out here.

"Emelie, what are you looking for?" calls Cora Jo.

"Hush up and help me look for shoes for Stephen. He's in dire need."

"Is what you're doing 'scavenging?'"

"I don't know what it is, but our brother is practically walking on the soles of his feet. He needs shoes."

I leave Cora Jo using her foot to move sticks, stones and soil away to better see what is partially hidden underneath.

"Thanks, Cora Jo," I say. We must find shoes for Stephen before we begin walking again."

I see a lump of clothing a short distance away from the rest of the group. As I get closer, it looks more like a lean-to with a canvas cover. I bend down to uncover the lump and feel something hard underneath. Eager to find shoes, I turn back the cloth and find myself staring at a cadaver. My scream comes as an instinct. I hear myself yell, but can't stop. Lawrence comes first and turns my whole body away from the dead young man. Soon everyone is around me and I can almost hear Bertie's voice saying, "Dear child, there is nothing to fear. It's just the face of death that took your own breath away. Imagine the pain of the family that had to leave him here."

I hear Papa. "Not having shovels there was nothing to do but leave him under the protection of these discards."

"Mama," says Cora Jo, "Emelie was trying to find shoes for Stephen. Did you see how worn his are?"

Mama comes to me with a sweet embrace. "Eugene, could you see if the young man still has shoes on his feet?"

I hear Papa moving about, but I still can't look.

"Here they are. What you were seeking, Emelie." Papa offers the shoes. I can't take them.

"Stephen, come here to try them. If they fit, they are a gift from your sister and this young man who is at rest."

As Mama holds me close, we all watch Stephen remove his ragged shoes and put the boy's own on his feet. After we prayed for his soul to be in eternal peace, we commence our journey. I stay close to Mama. I still need her strength to overcome the shock.

Not long after our walk began again, Stephen moves over to me. He puts his arm around my shoulders. I say nothing. Later, much later, he says "Thanks for the shoes. I love you, Emelie." I weep again, for I hadn't felt this close to my brother for a long time.

As we walk through this space, I pray it will be our last trial. I notice everything: the rock formations that look like giant toadstools, the deep blue of the sky that looks like the color of cool water, the sunburned reddish-brown faces of our wagon mates. I want to get this place into my mind so I will never forget how difficult survival can be.

For most of the trek we are silent, saving our speaking energy for walking and toting. One day we see our reward. There in the distance loom the Sierras, high and snow-capped. At their base we know is a stand of cottonwoods, too far to see yet, but Papa said the Truckee River was feeding them, a river that would be our source for water and food.

I tug at Lawrence and say, "We are going to the promised land of the Truckee River basin. Oh ye of little faith, be thankful."

He looks at me in his funny way and says, "It was me who had the faith. Celtic ways leave no room for fiddling with God."

"I never doubted, although sorrow was a heavy burden for me. I did pray for the safety of my family. Would it have been different had I prayed for everyone in our caravan? Would they have been safe? What about the others we don't know, the ones whose names are carved on the granite rock called Independence. We lost Tim, your beloved Mama, sister and young niece, then Luke, Sarah, and finally my dear Bertie. I feel the love of God most times, but when I'm in sorrow, I lose that feeling."

"That's when you need prayer most of all," he says to me. "The cupla focal keeps you attached to our God."

"The cupla focal? What's that?"

"A couple of words . . . . all you need is a couple of words. He'll hear you."

CHAPTER 24

California Territory

October, 1849

The first night in the Sierra Nevada Mountains are the coldest we have ever been on this journey. Clear, dry cold. Cora Jo and I huddle together to keep as warm as possible. At last there is a certain peace surrounding our wagon train knowing we had only eighty miles to go.

On the third day of the eighty-mile trek, the wagon wheels which had rolled across three thousand miles show their dryness, and the metal bar that held them together comes apart. As soon as Papa hears the tinny clanking sound, he stops our train.

We reorganize once again! From four wagons to three. Each wagon has three oxen. Milo and Maisy still carry the tenting and cooking equipment. We no sooner set out again when another wagon loses two of its wheels.

"Papa, don't you think we still have too much? You said the Sierras are higher than the Rockies were at the South Pass. We left our books at the first purge. What else can we leave right now, to make the ascent easier?" I say.

"Journals, pots, pans?" says Stephen.

"No, not ever the journals, Papa. We must keep them forever to remind us of all this traveling." I say.

"Has anyone else kept a written record of our traveling?" asks Papa.

"I believe we've been too busy just surviving," says Mama. "Emelie is the writer. Darling, if you can carry your journal it's yours to keep.

"We'll need blankets and water for sure," says David.

"Our knives and musket, too," Stephen says.

"Yes," says Papa. "Those weapons served Vince and Frank well. We shouldn't be without them."

Grandma Bertie's personal papers, still stored in her wooden box with the jade inlay, are carefully transferred to two knapsacks to be carried by Milo. As they are tied onto the mule, I remember our Grandma with such a feeling of emptiness that I quickly scan the trail ahead to keep my tears inside. There I see a granite wall out in the distance, shiny, white and strong, like our dear Bertie herself. She is with us through these last mountains.

"How will we scale this one, Papa?" asked Stephen.

"By dismantling the wagons. We'll use all three oxen to pull each wagon to the top," Papa says.

"It's going to be a steep incline. We may need to help the oxen ascend," says Vince.

"It may work if we tie ropes around each of the oxen, and then use our strength to pull on them, as they pull on the wagons. This will be a dandy to cross."

Once again, our group removes their scanty possessions from the wagons. I see the men, the oxen and the wagons being tied together for the climb up the steep-grade granite wall. It is frightening to watch the boys pushing the wagon from the rear and the men slipping on the rock ahead. As the men and boys slip, or their fingers become too bloody due to sharp edges in the rock, they bind them up and continue. Besides Papa, Lawrence, Stephen and David, others are waiting their turn to push or pull. By nightfall we had ascended about one mile by Papa's calculations.

"We're so close, yet so far," says Cora Jo. "Why is the hardest job near the end?"

"I know," I agree. "The hardest travel should be at the front end when we are all fresh and energetic. *Cupla focal* is all we need to pray, Cora Jo."

"What's that?"

"The couple of words that God hears. We don't need elaborate prayers for Him to hear us. Remember that when you become disheartened about things," I say.

We make camp on a narrow ridge. Our meager rations consist only of hard bread that was baked at the meadows. Mama soaks one end in vinegar to prevent scurvy because we had long been without fresh fruit or pickles. We had our water to drink. Our oxen, mules and horses are given the remainder of the plump grasses they had carried on their backs. Some did not seem so plump, but they had stayed green. Tonight we do not tie them because no one knows where they would be safe. Papa hopes that instinct will keep them away from the precipices.

Lawrence suggests the boys and men each put their blanket near an animal.

"Proximity to a human might keep them from moving about. Any slipping might cause fright among the others and even stampede up here in the high country."

Cora Jo, Mama and I sleep in a wagon. It is still dark when Cora Jo nudges me.

"I don't see Anoa," she whispers.

"Maybe she went down the hill away. Go back to sleep. Besides, I'm cold when you sit up, and Mama might hear us."

"But I'm worried about her. Please come with me."

I get up, pull a sweater over my dress, and slowly follow my sister out of the wagon onto the ledge. She points to a lump I can barely see.

"That must be her, asleep," she says, as she disappears quickly in the predawn darkness to get a closer look.

"Emelie," she screams, "she's dead, she's dead!"

I run over to her and see Anoa, lying down sideways, her stomach slit, blood still pouring out.

"What's going on there?" calls Papa from his sleep mat.

"Oh, Papa! Anoa is dead! She's been shot with an arrow," I call out.

Soon the whole camp is awake. As the eastern sky turns purple in preparation for sunrise, the group sees that Anoa had been shot for her organs. They had been carefully removed as only the Diggers knew how to do.

"I read about his kind of attack," Papa says. "When Diggers kill an animal in a caravan, they keep the prized portions: the heart, liver and kidneys for themselves. The rest they leave for us to eat. If we cannot eat it all, they return and enjoy it after our caravan has left the area."

"No sense wasting this meat," says Mama. "Let's boil up some to sustain us for this mountain trek."

"Mama, we have no pots or kettles," I remember.

"We'll roast it over an open pit, then," says Mama, and we all disperse to find bits of bushes and brush.

Lawrence finds a piece of branch large enough for a spit. Papa and the other men carve out the tenderloin for roasting. Blood dripping, it goes on the spit, and soon the odor of the roasting meat along with the coldness of the morning stimulates the appetites of our small group.

I know my sister will not touch a morsel of the meat no matter how hungry she might be. She mopes and weeps as one does when a friend leaves. Stephen and David are very gentle with her and speak about owning a ranch or farm with animals she could care for.

It takes two more days before the summit is reached, and it is not until that moment when Cora Jo lifts from her sadness. We are 10,500 feet high and pockets of pure, white snow surround us. The fresh water it provides quenches us, as we eagerly stuff it into our mouths.

Papa says it is a miracle we had come so high without an accident, for some of the portions of the wall were very icy. Mama reminds us of the small prayer which we all repeat as we stand there: *"In the name of the Father and the Son and the Holy Ghost. Amen."*

The other miracle was the view from the downside of the Sierras. It was green! There were thickets of dense trees. Birds were fluttering about, singing, and squirrels were scampering everywhere. It was like springtime after a bitter winter except that the harshness we had endured had come from desert heat and the cold mountains rather than a change of season.

Boulders are scattered about the slope and they are like the best seats at a circus. We all sit to enjoy the breathtaking sight before us when Papa calls Cora Jo, the boys, Mama and me to his side.

"We made it, my precious family. Here we are, looking at California!"

Then, as if the moment is too strong to be contained within our small group, we jump up and hug everyone in sight. It was a New Year's celebration, a birthday and Christmas all over again. There is shouting, yelling, laughing and weeping. There is dancing, right there on the summit, too. We hook our arms and kick our tired legs into the air.

As Lawrence hugs me close, I feel as Papa did way back home. This IS a time of new beginnings. Before us lay lush land, perhaps gold, and new people to meet. Instinctively I feel for the dough heart. It has been long gone, but that doesn't matter. It kept me strong as I traveled this journey. Aden will always be in my heart. He is the tie to my past. I will always have my memories, but the todays and tomorrows in my life are where I want to live. At last I can say that I have seen the *elephant* and survived it. The *elephant* is not the gold. I know now that the *elephant* is the hardship, sickness, deaths and hurts we have endured. This I know as my own name. I smile in this knowing while my tears flow freely as the rivers I had crossed on this journey.

END

WAGON TRAIN CAKE (NO EGGS, NO MILK)

2 c. raisins
2 c. brown sugar
2 ½ c. water
1 c. shortening
2 tsp. cinnamon
1 tsp. nutmeg
2 tsp. baking soda
3 ½ c. flour
1 tsp. salt
1 c. walnuts

Mix them all together and bake.

BIBLIOGRAPHY

Research for *West* was conducted through many books, some only available at university libraries and others from public libraries.

Adams, Henry. *The United States in 1800.* Ithaca, NY: Cornell University Press, 1979.

Brown, Henry B. *Old New York: Yesterday & Today.* New York: Valentine's Manual, 1922.

Horan, Julie L. *The Porcelain God.* Secaucus, NY: Carol Publishing Group, 1997.

Peavy, L. & Smith, U. *Frontier Women.* New York: Barnes and Noble Books, 1996.

Rosenberg, Charles E. *The Cholera Years.* Chicago: University of Chicago Press, 1971.

Schlissel, Lillian. *Women's Diaries of the Westward Journey.* New York: Schocken Books, 1982.

BIOGRAPHY

Growing up in the borough of Queens in New York City, my best friend and I would sit on the quad of Queens College and gaze with dream filled eyes at the skyline of New York. It was a city I never experienced fully, to my regret. After teaching in both Mineola and Elmont School Districts in Nassau County, I left the area, and became involved in funded educational research projects with young children. With the completion of an Ed.D. program at the University of Florida, I taught at both the College of William and Mary and the Florida State University, directed the Visitor Center at NASA Langley, and eventually returned to classroom teaching at Lee Hall Elementary in Newport News, Virginia.

Made in United States
North Haven, CT
29 August 2024

56696105R00096